MOVE UP, JOHN

D0608935

MOVE UP, JOHN

by
Fionn
MacColla

*edited and
introduced by
John Herdman*

CANONGATE
PRESS
EDINBURGH 1994

Published by Canongate Press Ltd, 14 Frederick Street, Edinburgh EH2 2HB. © Mary MacDonald 1994. Introduction © John Herdman 1994.

The publishers acknowledge subsidy from the Scottish Arts Council towards the publication of this volume

Book design by Dogand Bone, Glasgow.

British Library Cataloguing-in-Publication Data
A catalogue record for this book is available on request from the British Library

ISBN 0 86241 381 8

Typeset by The Electronic Book Factory Ltd, Fife, Scotland. Printed and bound in Great Britain by Cromwell Press Ltd, Broughton Gifford, Melksham, Wiltshire.

Contents

257-2

Where conversations are not obviously in Braid Scots (called English up till the century of this book) it is ti be understood that they are in the Scottish or Gaelic language.
—Fionn MacColla

To J. O.

INTRODUCTION

BY JOHN HERDMAN

THE HISTORY of the composition and vicissitudes of *Move Up, John* is somewhat complicated and requires elucidation. The novel, written mostly in Benbecula, where Fionn MacColla was a headmaster, between 1941 and 1946, represented the culmination of its author's engagement with a complex of cultural, philosophical and religious issues which had already preoccupied him for a number of years and had found partial expression in his previous novels *The Albannach* (1932) and *And The Cock Crew* (1945).

In his new work, set in sixteenth-century Scotland, MacColla sought to penetrate to the root causes of the Reformation within the soul of man and to point to what he believed were its disastrous consequences for subsequent Scottish history and the evolution of the Scottish psyche. Years later, in *At the Sign of the Clenched Fist* (1967), he described it as 'a novel of the dramatic type, in which the characters, representing the various elements involved in the Reformation in Scotland, acted and reacted upon each other and so wove a pattern of events which ought to have described the course of the movement and, one hoped, disclosed its nature.' He insisted, too, that it was 'a novel used as a method of enquiry, not . . . a novel written to a thesis.'[1] Elsewhere he observed that his purpose was 'to write a novel which would have the effect of *showing* the reader what *really* happened at the Reformation, knowing only too well that to *argue* the thing out would be merely to arouse a furious opposition of

conditioned emotions with rationalisations galore to justify
them.'2

In spite of several revisions and rewritings, *Move Up,
John* failed to find a publisher, and a pattern of rejection
and frustration was established which was to dog MacColla
for the rest of his writing life. 'I was very naive of course,'
he wrote later, 'if I ever expected that novel to be published
as a novel. The days are long gone by when the public will
tolerate being edified by a novelist, or indeed being edified
at all by any kind of writer.'3 This does not quite tell the
whole story, however, for it is clear that MacColla had
his own doubts as to the structural and aesthetic viability
of his novel. When, years later, he was re-assembling
the parts of *Move Up, John* as constituent elements
within that non-fictional elucidation of its philosophical
argument which became *At the Sign of the Clenched
Fist*, he wrote a note headed 'The new Move Up, John',
evidently intended as a possible explanatory preface. This
note, to be found among the novelist's papers, reads as
follows:

> I tried by means of a novel to crash through a certain
> situation to the reality behind it. I think I reached the
> reality but in doing so the novel was smashed. As I
> don't think it could he reassembled in aesthetically
> satisfying shape I am hoping the public will accept
> the fragments so arranged as to help towards the
> apprehension of the reality in question.4

These doubts, elaborated upon at some length elsewhere among the writer's notes, are undoubtedly coloured
by MacColla's experience of rejection; in later years he
tended to be defensively casual in his references to his
unpublished work, affecting to be vague about the title
of *Move Up, John* and even claiming to have forgotten

the existence of the novel published post-humously as *The Ministers* (1979).[5] Equally, however, Mac Colla did believe that his creativity had been stunted and frustrated by the experience of teaching in the Outer Isles where he was continually bogged down among trivialities and forced against his will to participate in the de-Gaelicising of his pupils, their alienation through education from an irreplaceable cultural heritage. Later he was to describe these years as 'a never-ending horror of totally schizoid activity', and to speak in the same context of 'the deliberate stifling and strangling of my speculative and creative talent in which I had perforce to engage practically continuously'.[6]

It was, in fact, the conflict between the 'creative' and 'speculative' elements of his talent which constituted MacColla's central artistic dilemma, and to which he obliquely refers in the note quoted above. The compulsion which he felt to communicate the insights at which he had arrived, his restless sense of their overmastering urgency, exerted a pressure upon the novel form through which he sought to make them concrete, which broke down the restraints of traditional narrative structure. I have elsewhere considered at some length the effects of this dilemma in relation to *Move Up, John*[7]; this is not the place to repeat these arguments. Here it is sufficient to say that while the novel may not achieve a fully realised dramatic unity (consisting as it does of a series of magnificent set-pieces welded together by speculative passion rather than by the tenuous thread of narrative continuity), nonetheless its largeness of conception, the power and mastery of its language, its psychological penetration and its intellectual authority and coherence give it a kind of fractured greatness which is worth a hundred small successes.

In 1958 the second chapter of *Move Up, John* (not the

first, as stated by MacColla in the Foreword to *Ane Tryall of Heretiks*,[8] but the first of the four big 'set-piece' chapters) was issued by Castle Wynd Printers, Edinburgh, as a small separate edition under the title *Scottish Noël*. This vividly and passionately rendered account of a sixteenth-century battle was saluted by such critics as Edwin Muir, Naomi Mitchison and Sydney Goodsir Smith as marking the re-emergence of a major talent silent for too long. In 1962 the dramatic qualities of the third chapter were strikingly attested to when it was presented as *Ane Tryall of Heretiks* by the Curetes in the Paperback Bookshop during the Edinburgh Festival – a performance whose success inspired Jim Haynes with the idea that resulted in the Traverse Theatre; it was issued as a pamphlet the same year by Michael Slains of Collieston. In 1967 *Ane Tryall*, together with its Foreword, was reproduced in whole in *At the Sign of the Clenched Fist*, while significant portions of the remaining two of the four major chapters were further incorporated by MacColla as part of the structure of that work's philosophical argument. In all, perhaps something between a half and two-thirds of the original novel has been published in this fragmented form.

Move Up, John was left by MacColla in several incomplete drafts and revisions, and in one complete typed text with hand-written revisions. The version prepared for the various separate publications is the most recent, but an incomplete, recension. The latter differs from the first, completed version in a number of respects. In *Scottish Noël*, finding the cowardice or nervousness of his protagonist John Tod (the name substituted in early revision for the original John Rough) – the priest who becomes a Reformer – a distracting irrelevance within the new context of a self-contained episode, MacColla 'discarded him for the occasion and replaced him with another priest of identical outward appearance but very different military instincts.'⁹ This priest was called John Erskine. In *Scottish Noël* and the other separately published sections, the anti-Reforming priest Huisjean MacUalraig becomes Ninian Kennedy, 'Huisjean' heing a phonetic approximation of the Gaelic Uisdean (Hugh), while the Gaelic name MacUalraig is usually rendered in English by Kennedy. In the present edition, by agreement with Mrs. Mary MacDonald, MacColla's widow, the names John Tod and Uisdean MacUalraig are used.

While preparing his novel for fragmented publication, MacColla took the opportunity of making a number of further stylistic revisions and improvements; these are most extensive in *Scottish Noël*. In addition, in the interest of ready communicability of his ideas, which had increasingly come to seem to him a paramount consideration, he considerably modified the Scots he had originally used in speech in the direction of more anglicised forms and more contemporary usage and idiom. Thus he often (but not always) replaced "aa" by "all", "whilk" by "which", "nocht" by "not".

In 1977 the Scottish Arts Council made funds available to support editorial work on MacColla's unpublished texts. I undertook to edit *Move Up, John* along lines agreed with Mrs. MacDonald. In the case of the chapter which had become *Scottish Noël* it was, of course, necessary to reinstate John Tod in place of John Erskine, while retaining the other modifications made by the author to the original text; this involved some problems of disentanglement, but not insuperable ones.

The most difficult decisions related to MacColla's use of Scots. Mrs. MacDonald is clear that it was never, even in the early versions, the author's intention to reproduce authentic sixteenth-century Scots. His object was to use the Scots tongue in such a way as to combine communicability to the modern reader with the imparting of a flavour of the times in which his novel was set. Writing of the dramatic production of *Ane Tryall of Heretiks*, he spoke of its language as 'an only partially modernised version of the language in which the original debates would have been carried on had they taken place.'[10] Nor did he aim at complete internal consistency within any of the versions, and that, I am convinced, for good reasons. Different characters are made to employ different linguistic registers according to their character, temperament, social background and so on, and individual characters may speak differently on various occasions, depending on the degree of formality of the context in which they are speaking, or the degree of concreteness or abstraction in what they are saying. In preparing this edition I have respected this variety of practice. MacColla wrote not as a linguistic scholar or propagandist but as an artist with an exceptionally sensitive grasp of the living function of language as communication, and I believe that his instincts and judgment on these matters were sound.

It may be appropriate here to underline the point made in the author's prefatory note: dialogue which is to be understood as spoken in Gaelic (called 'Scottish' by MacColla) is *rendered* by standard English, all other dialogue being in some form of Scots. No conversations are to be understood as having been conducted in English.

I should like to thank Mr. Derrick McClure for his generous help and advice, and in conclusion to thank Mary MacDonald for her unfailing helpfulness and co-operation during the time when I was editing *Move Up, John*, and for undertaking the immense labour of typing the completed text. Her vivid memory, scrupulous attention to detail, kindliness and courtesy have made this editor's task a happy one indeed. Without her unstinting devotion to MacColla's work it is unthinkable that this novel would be appearing at all, fifty years after its author began to write it.

– January 1994.

REFERENCES

1. *At the Sign of the Clenched Fist*, Edinburgh 1967, p. 57.
2. 'Mein Bumpf,' in *Essays on Fionn MacColla*,
              editor David Morrison, Thurso 1973, p. 28.
3. *At the Sign of the Clenched Fist*, p. 58
4. National Library of Scotland, Deposit No. 239.
5. *Essays on Fionn MacColla*, pp. 28, 29.
6. Ibid, pp. 27, 28.
7. 'Fionn MacColla: Art and Ideas,'
              in *Cencrastus* no. 13, Summer 1983.
    8. *At the Sign of the Clenched Fist*, p. 71.
      9. Ibid., p. 69   **10.** Ibid, p. 70.

TWO PRIESTS

MOVE UP, JOHN 1

PART ONE

THE TWO MEN IN CLERICAL DRESS sat looking at each other. On the table between them a meal lay unregarded. In the window the light of day was failing fast, and every instant the candles burning at the end of the board brought out more clearly a whiteness in their faces. A manservant was standing across the room looking at them. A rigidity in his posture suggested the effect of sudden shock.

Outside in the street a commotion was going on. There was running of feet, calling of alarmed voices, some crying out of women, the occasional clink of arms. By contrast the stillness in the room stood heavy and unbroken: nothing moved except the shadows when a draught set the candles flickering.

One of the men at the table was tall and broad-shouldered, with a strong, well-covered frame, about thirty-five. His features which would normally wear a look of open frankness were relaxed and expressionless, the naturally firm jaw limp and fallen. His blue eyes were wide on his companion, but with a sort of intermittence of vision, as if the mind behind came only from time to time to look outward and retired again to turn upon some private thoughts within. He sat squarely to the table, his arms spread out sideways and hands resting on the table's edge, staring across at the other with that intermittently unseeing glance, while the silence lengthened, the gleam out of doors faded away, and the shadows darkened into solid forms beyond the candle-light.

The other, opposite him, was both striking-looking and insignificant. He was under the average size, and of no great force of body. But the bright close mat of his fiery red hair made a startling effect against the pallor of the narrow face below. And out of the face – most arresting feature of all – deep-set under thick brows of a lighter colour than the hair, glowed his eyes. Those dark brown eyes were fixed with a kind of burning expression on his bigger companion, steadily, although seeming somehow as if always about to give an apprehensive flicker sideways or backwards. He held his hands out of sight in his lap, and there was a suggestion about his shoulders of being hunched, and about his head of being drawn down between them, as if he had just been missed by a blow. One could sense his tension.

The commotion outside was dying away, in sudden stages. The cries and exclamations scattered, became fewer, ceased: the last footsteps scurried out of hearing. Not a sound. A sort of numbness fallen, as if over the whole country. The fire could be heard burning.

A whisper came from the bigger man . . ."Is it . . . is it true, think ye, John?"

The small man with the red hair never relaxed his attitude or the tenseness of his gaze. A minute passed. Suddenly . . . "It maun be!" he exclaimed, and the bigness of his voice was a surprise.

The silence settled again.

The bigger man had raised his eyes and was gazing

away past him into the far shadows of the room with a kind of speculative intensity. "The Cardinal!" he whispered . . . "*The Cardinal!*"

With a harsh sudden movement he thrust back his chair as if to rise. But he only placed a hand on each knee, and looking fixedly across at the little red-haired man said in angry, outraged tones: "It's the traitors, John! Lippen on it, it's Henry's tools! It's the heretics!"

They stared again at each other: the big man flushed, his blue eyes flashing, the smaller yet more tensed together, whiter of face. No sound came from out-of-doors, only the same palpability of the silence. They might have been listening for the first breath of the dawn of doom.

"They ha' finished the Cardinal. I wonder . . . what mair than the Cardinal hae they finished?" The tall man's anger had died already: his sad tone was a reflective questioning . . . "An the traitors have their will now . . . I trow it will be *finis Scotiae!*"

The little red-haired man had never altered his position; but his fright had been subtly passing, and into the expression of his burning eyes – moved away now from his companion's face and fixed on the distance beyond – was creeping a look . . . almost like feverish speculation. All at once he seemed seized with strong excitement. An exclamation escaped his lips. "The douncome!" he almost shouted, gazing before him into space.

Suddenly he shouted in earnest – "*The douncome!*" – his great voice filling the room.

He jumped up and stood, at his insignificant height, tensed, yet as if in a dream.

With some jerkiness both of limbs and features, coming partly to himself, he strode across the floor and picking up a candlestick with an unlighted candle came back and held it to one of those burning at the end of the board. The tall man, startled by his actions and sudden exclamations, was taking close note of him as he stood directly opposite and so near at hand. The little man's brown eyes were lit up by the candles shining directly into the deep sockets under the thick reddish brows. He was abstracted, watching the flame broaden and pass from one candle to the other, his hair a bright halo around his pale narrow brow. The light showed up a number of large irregularly-shaped freckles under the pale skin, and strained lines about his mouth. The whiteness of the breast and especially the seams of the worn, once-black cassock showed painfully. One became aware of him as a living, breathing body, so near, inside the threadbare cassock. And the hands with their covering of dry, whitish hair; small and somewhat claw-like. The restlessness of the thin lips betrayed the excitement still in him.

His candle was alight. With an absent-minded, habitual movement, he made the sign of the cross upon his breast and turning abruptly without a word strode across the room and disappeared behind a door.

2

AS a matter of fact he had had no recollection while lighting his candle that anyone else was present. On coming into his own chamber he closed the door, set down the candle, and clasping his hands behind him began pacing restlessly up and down, pressing his lips together.

He was in a very strange state. The more strange in that he did not understand its composition, or how it had come to possess him. (Not that he was by any means a stranger to such states.) The first effect of the news of the Cardinal's murder had been to stun him: the next, when his faculties began to recover, panic.

The Cardinal was the prop of all. One moveless point in a shifting world, of legendary fixity. In those days of armed enemies without the realm and riding by night of traitors and heretics within, a rock in the general mind against perturbation. His unerring eye above taken for granted, and his ability to bring to naught the schemes of plotters against public order and the small man's peace. The Cardinal! What troubles and dangers, terrors and uncertainties would not wing down upon the dweller in the land now he was done away! No wonder the mind was whelmed in the expectancy and for a time refused its function.

Yet when the schoolmaster out there, Uisdean Mac-Ualraig, had asked that question, 'Is it true, think ye, John?' something from his lowermost depths was stirred into rising up, struggling up, in contradiction of the grain of doubt implied. He had said, 'It *maun* be' – as if he had *wanted* it to be. And though in truth he had never wanted it – the murder; never thought – could not have thought – of wanting it, or anything so thunderous and alarming, yet when he said the words, 'It maun be', he had felt all at once for a single moment that he *did* want it and *had* wanted it, even that this was precisely what he had all along been wanting. Or that something in him, or of him, had been wanting.

Yes, and it was so now. He could hear now the sub-terranean approving voice, which he vehemently wished silent, yet applauded even while – for the sake of his peace, and because its boldness frightened him – he could have silenced it.

With it, with that voice, went in some unclear way connected the wind of triumph, of speculation-tinged excitement, like exhilaration, that immediately after swept through his breast and mind. And went on surging there.

His breast was seething, his mind on fire, with some
unrecognised anticipation. He was on fire with some
untracked 'possibility'. He would have grasped it, so that
he might look at it, for it made a war in him: a battle of two
wills – two armies of desires both carrying his own device,
one armoured with a habitude of darkness, fighting with a
silent point – and always an unhappy skirmish of misgiving
out upon the flanks. And it eluded him. Even as he seemed
about to seize it, gliding from him in obscurity. Yet (he felt)
down in that lowermost whence the bold voice spoke he
understood, and knew the commander's name of those
dark regiments. How could that name reverberate in the
depths yet be unechoed in the upper 'he'? Strangely . . .
and this misgave him . . . ever as he called down to know
that name it gave him back his own!

How torturing this state – against-ness and the fear
of an unknown approaching; disapproved approval and
wild hope of its approach: horror and triumph warring
together, with circumambient qualms of guilt!

A word had come from him out there – 'the douncome'. He had known what it meant, and did not know
what it meant . . . the warcry of the armies from the
depths! Their warcry – 'the douncome!' What they had
wanted, what he had wanted, or something deep down
within him wanted, was 'the douncome!' Some portion
of overhanging guilt departed from him then, perceiving
that all the uprising within – triumph, approval, and
anticipation – had accompanied after all not the murder,
but 'the douncome'. But what douncome?

What had he meant by it? 'The douncome'.

3

UISDEAN MACUALRAIG, in the outer room, was
puzzled about him.

He had not moved except to rest his right elbow on the table-edge and crook his forefinger about his chin; and there he sat, solid rather than bulky, looking at the door through which the small, red-haired man had vanished in such haste, setting the shadows in a quaking dance about the room a second later when the draught had flicked the candles. His actions had been strange, strange enough to attract the notice even in such a moment of larger preoccupation. Yes, and even before the shout and excited movements, one had been aware through the stupor of the mind of a something inappropriate to the occasion in the expression of those burning dark-brown eyes. It came to him now. There should not have been a *speculation* there. They might have been horror-stricken, or wondering, but their speculating look was out of keeping. Jarring, some-how. And the excitement that sprang up in him! And that shout – 'the douncome! ' What was agitating the man?

An unquiet spirit, John. Gusted upon with moods within. In spite of that habitual tensedness or near-rigidity over the whole man, the pale mask-like face especially, one knew the humours come and go. The thin lips at least were not controlled, or the restless hands. And the eyes, those strange eyes, blazed all abroad. One might be talking with him, on some common theme, or calmly with him merely – and suddenly, from no apparent where, know the mood go through him. And the eyes blaze up upon you. Sometimes an inscrutable look; sometimes a look as like as might be to malice concentrate. It would take one aback. Ever inconstant, he might seem friendly perhaps, yet when one's disposition went out to him, of a sudden, incomprehensibly, one knew him become hard-elbowed and averted. A disturbing man, John. One tried to hold him brotherly, in charity and patience. He had aye been so: frigid and yet tempestuous. Or had he been?

His memory went back some five and twenty years. Maister Scot, the dominie, seated upon his stool. Virgil. The musty schoolroom smell. The door opens a little way and the bird-like head of Canon Kyle appears. He nods in his bird-like way to the master on his stool. Maister Scot, the jocular, nods back, with the faintest suggestion of an imitation of the other. The class titters. Canon Kyle withdraws his head, the door opens a little wider, a boy with a head of flaming hair comes in, trots into the centre of the floor. He is too young, they think: no, at a second glance his face is as old as theirs: he is undergrown. He has the rather pale face that goes with his hair colouring, but he looks well-fed. Contemptuous glances are cast upon his clothes: they are thick – and too many; he has the appearance of being padded. Somebody whispers: Mother's dearie! The class titters. The boy is standing, planted in stout, new boots, smiling in a self-complacent way and casting around the rows an interested, curious glance from remarkable dark-brown eyes.

Father Scot on his stool is eyeing him in the mock-solemn way they all know well. There is a movement of anticipation. At length he says, booming in Latin, "What seekest thou here?" – and, as if by an afterthought – "Elijah!" The class laugh . . . and suddenly the laugh rises to a roar that shakes the room, and goes on, endlessly, ever renewed. The boy on the floor, whether through ignorance of Latin or inattention to the question, or having his thoughts elsewhere, has answered . . . "John Tod!" And that is nothing: his voice . . . his voice is as big as the master's own! When the roar goes up he beams round upon them. When it goes on he begins to laugh himself. At this the roar grows louder. He roars also. The class is in paroxysms . . . still he goes on roaring. But suddenly there had been a moment: he stops, looks at the class doubtfully, at the master, whose gravity is apparently undisturbed; at the class once more. For a moment he seems on the point of laughing again. Then a puzzled frown, an expression of pain, appears on his brow: he casts a sort of anxious searching look along the rows of laughers. All at once his face changes. One look half pleading, half reproachful at the class and his eyes fall. He has become deathly pale. Only the coarser sort among the scholars go on laughing. The master claps his hands and calls for silence.

It is a different boy now, out on the floor. All the self-assurance has gone from him. He seems all at once to have become small inside his over-thick clothes. When the master points to a bench and tells him to go and sit there he looks up dumbly, then goes with a slow step, his eyes cast down. He sits on the wrong bench, its occupants shuffling up with alacrity to give him room. There he sits, looking on the ground. He shivers. The master begins reading rapidly in Latin and the work of the class is going on again. After a while nudges are passing round. It is seen that John Tod is crying . . .

For a week thereafter no one saw him: it was supposed that he would not return. Then one day he reappeared, the same clothes and boots but a different John Tod. He slipped in at the assembling of the class with face averted, avoiding observation, and during the whole lesson never raised his eyes. When the class broke up he was of course surrounded and they began to tease him. They were asking him in chorus: What seekest thou here? And calling him 'the Prophet'. He made no reply, turned away his face, and struggled to escape: and breaking free at last ran off quickly. When they grew accustomed to seeing his red head in the class and passing in and out they gradually left off teasing, all but a few. John Tod perked up again. He began tentatively to push himself forward, seeking notice. But with complete unsuccess. His personality proved too aggressive for companions; the few who might have taken up with him, out of compassion more than anything, soon found him domineering and demanding, and passed him by. Then he tried to shine. In their sports and games, but he was too puny; they were all stronger than he. In studies – he applied himself with assiduity – but it was soon apparent his gifts were mediocre. In all their activities he found himself passed over, with indifference or contempt. One would come upon him in some corner: he would turn his face to the wall, his hands clenched and eyes full of tears. He began to wrap himself up, to grow his shell.

A certain kind of boy would have gone on baiting him. But he found a means of defending himself. At first he had merely turned aside his eyes and tried to slip away. But once, in a corner, pressed beyond measure, he lifted up a roaring voice and poured out such a flood of words as appeared to amaze even himself. His tormentor drew back: some said he even grew pale. Ever after a would-be victimiser had to reckon with his growing fluency. He would tuck in his chin and thrusting his shoulder forward drown his antagonist in a torrent of furious invective uttered in a deafening voice. His greatest potency was in calling down calamities in grisly multitude upon his persecutors. The hearers flinched, and cast a look upon him. Many were afraid of him, and even the hardiest learned to avoid the anger of 'the Prophet'.

It was so that he began to be what he had ever since remained. He grew into a little flaming-haired man with a strut, a consequential air – and a tremendous voice; with a cold exterior and pale, mask-like face, the glance habitually lowered with what might have been humility, but at times uncovering his burning eyes in a look as of malice or contempt that made one feel uneasy. It had become so much his settled personality that years ago one learned to accept him in it, and scarce remembered him with any other . . .

But the other thing – the dire calamity – had all this time like an arctic area at the back of consciousness been attempting to push forward fingers of icy depression, and these lengthening fully now, closed like a hand over Uisdean MacUalraig's mind. That dastard act had as it were dropped an impenetrable curtain not an inch before the eyes, blocking hope, and hope in time; a curtain black like sin, like treason and all unnatural distortions of the unregenerate human will, drenched with the Cardinal's blood and the blood of martyred honour. He saw innocence, the true heart, outraged in the ages . . . war and confusion to men of good will . . . the filthy spittle of crude avarice and ignorant malice on God's image, the citadel of honour in the human soul . . . He turned and for a time, as if struck by something about him, looked very attentively at the manservant, still standing rigidly there by the wall, looking at him. A very ordinary-looking man . . . waiting for him to speak. But Uisdean MacUalraig, after looking at him intently as if pondering some thought or consideration that had come into his mind about him, sighed and with a slight shaking of the head turned away.

After a little he roused himself and got up as if to go towards the door . . . But he could not get John Tod out of his mind either. There was something that profoundly disturbed him about the little man's behaviour, his strange actions and exclamations, in the context of this catastrophic event. A strange personality. Especially for a priest. Somehow not at all a priest-like personality. Very strange that after having known him for most of a lifetime and living in the same house with him for years one never yet thought naturally of him as a priest. Even before the altar he was John Tod in vestments. Was he then, like some others, a man out of his true place, not really called to the priesthood? One tried to picture him in any secular walk of life – a baxter, wright, or candlemaker. No, one could see him chafing intolerably in his station. A merchant then? Yes, perhaps a merchant; a merchant was best of all. One could see him as a merchant, and by dint of aggression and his dominating voice the master of his guild. Yet a priest fitted him too, better than anything. Yet not a priest, but something like a priest. Something or other like a priest, yet not a priest . . .?

He had taken a few steps towards the door when the manservant stood away from the wall behind him.

"You'd be the better of taking your meat, Master Uisdean," he said in the Scottish language with a note of solicitude.

Uisdean MacUalraig merely stopped long enough, without turning, to incline his head.

"Good to you, *'ghille* . . . no meat for me. I'm to my prayers."

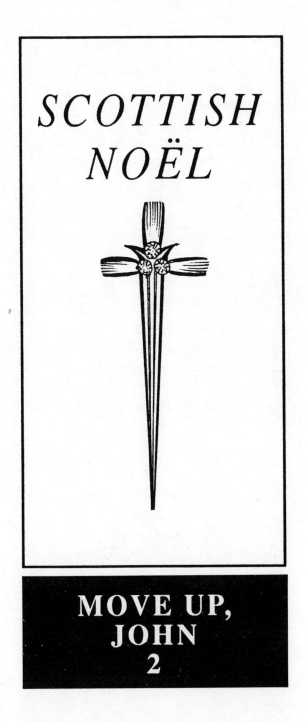

SCOTTISH
NOËL

**MOVE UP,
JOHN
2**

PART TWO

WHO BRINGETH LIGHT AT MIDNIGHT. WHO MAKETH A PATH IN DARKNESS. WHO COVERETH THE WHOLE EARTH WITH PURITY AS WITH A GARMENT, AND MEN SING HIS PRAISES RISING IN THE NIGHT. WHOSE HEART MAKETH A CONVERSATION OF LOVE BETWEEN HEART AND HEART, AND MEN HASTEN FROM THEIR DOORS IN THE NAME OF LOVE. WHOSE SWEETNESS FILLS THE AIR.

WHO STILLS THE VOICE OF THE WORLD, MAKING A HUSH WHERE MANY ARE. WHO IS GREAT THAT LIETH IN LITTLENESS, A SON AND FATHERS BOW DOWN BEFORE HIM. WHO IS INNOCENCE THAT BREAKS THE HEART, AND RENEWING OF HOPE, BEFORE WHOM SORROW GIVETH PLACE TO JOY. WHOSE PRAISE IS A HARMONY SOARING AND LOFTY.

WHO IS HOLINESS AND THE HUMILITY OF THOSE THAT BOW THE KNEE. WHO IS COME, AND HIS COMING NOW IS THE EXPECTATION OF ALL. TO WHOM IS MADE THE OFFERING OF HEARTS . . .

There is a passing to the right, a flutter of vestments, a moving across to leftwards.

Master John Tod has mounted to the pulpit. When he uncovers his head it seems in its brightness to add one to the company of the angels under the roof and the saints standing in their niches.

The Gospel of the Mass is taken from the holy Gospel according to St. Luke, chapter two: *Joseph gaed up from Galilee to Bethlehem in Judea with Mary his espousit wife, and her days being accomplishit she brocht forth her first-born son and wrappit him in swaddling claiths and layit him in a manger. And the angel of the Lord appearit to shepherds watching their sheep and sayit unto them: Fear not, for behold I bring you guid tidings of great joy, that sall be to all people, for this day is born to you a Saviour, whilk is Christ the Lord.* But he takes his text from the Lesson of the Mass, which is from the Epistle of St Paul the Apostle to Titus, chapter two: *The grace of God our Saviour hath appearit to all men, instructing us, that denying ungodliness and wordly desires, we should live soberly, and justly and godly in this world.*

'Ungodliness and worldly desires!' He seems immediately to become incensed with somebody, and in the sound of his trumpeting the dew of peace is turned into a rain of wrath. The indignation in his voice returns to him quivering from the walls and roof, and makes him in turn indignant. He soars upwards on it. Out of the partial gloom the faces are turned attentively, riveted by a voice. And the voice is his. The sound, though it fills the building, is no greater than his swelling consciousness. He rises with its volume till he is become no common vessel, but a man sent. It is for him all those have come, and his resounding words. He reads his warrant in their paling faces. They are compelled to listen . . . cannot not listen . . . to his thunder, while he plays upon them like an organ. As the roof resounds the more, he rises more unlimited, and calls forth on them the greater loudness of a paler hue. Till when he feels them shudder his unfettered being floats upon the sounding air . . .

'In the name of the Father, and of the Son, and of the Holy Ghost.'

He turns to descend . . . Uisdean MacUalraig is sitting down there in the sanctuary in his vestments, hands on knees, not looking at him. Uisdean MacUalraig is big, and round and strong, unruffable within and a heady scholar. He is, for all that, but an *ordinary* man, and waits to be John Tod's assistant . . . John Tod has descended now from the pulpit, passes, dipping, from custom, before the altar, vests, is conducted back, all as in a dream. And in the o'erhang of a dream remounts the altar and begins the Creed . . .

But now as he proceeds with that part of the Mass called the Offertory the vapour of his dream begins to waver and be blown upon by a familiar anticipation never yet identified . . . There is some reluctance in him, not to be shaken off: his hands above the altar are growing heavy . . . The clashing of a bell behind him evokes a sickness and anxiety, and immediately the urgency of an impulse takes the form of thinking he hears feet – his own feet – retreating in a panic scamper. His hands are become as heavy as lead.

'*For. . . this. . . is. . . My. . . Body. . .*'

He had cast himself headlong down before the altar, hiding his face, striving to grovel from sight while he cried out, *Holy, holy, holy* with shrieks and smitings of the breast. At the same time, and with absolute simultaneity, he was flying backwards, pushing out his hands in front, with reeling eyes, crying, *Nay, I cannot, I cannot!* Then

he was turning and rushing out of the church – even after
he had reached the open air, struggling with his hands
upstretched against the weight of something that pressed
down upon his head and shoulders, threatening to crush
him utterly to dust and nothing . . . In reality he was
standing still before the altar, shaken and oblivious: in
the hush of the elements listening to the storm within,
mounting up, shrieking, blotting out the world.

Presently he knew again where he was, and what in
act of doing. But still the tempest raged apace within: and
suddenly it was injected with a stream of hot intemperate
feeling from below, staining all other components of the
conflict with a furious red. The end was that, failing other
outlet, he finished saying Mass with his mind averted from
the meaning of all he said and did – yet as it were averting
it from that averting of it. So strong and insuperable the
tension in him of strange contending opposites that he
could scarcely tell whether he bowed when he ought to
bow or retained himself erect. Sometimes it even seemed
that he did both at once.

As he came from the altar he saw nothing of the
people standing. A sense was in him as of some sacrilege,
a guilty awe: at the same time a sense of deprivation, of
having been . . . of having been *robbed*. And mingling
with them . . . and rising to the mastery . . . a burning
deep resentment.

2

UISDEAN MacUalraig came out of the church and
casting a casual glance about noticed that already the
last worshippers had passed from sight. From the left,
in the direction of the market-place, came slightly but
clearly on the frosty air the diminishing sound of footsteps
in the snow. The night was piercing cold. From the house

roofs right up and over the near-full moon spread a vast luminous net spangled innumerably with swimming motes. In the tingling air one seemed to hear a distant singing.

He walked a few paces to the right where there was some garden ground, cold and deserted, with irregularities of upturned soil under thin snow, and solitary vegetable stalks, motionless, each holding up a white puffed head. Beyond, the glance passed unimpeded to southward, over rolling, rising country, till it reached low hills. In the west stood motionless snow-clouds, towering masses glittering like sparkling fleece all along their upper edge, but turning a heavy face of lead-coloured surface towards the earth. To the left above the house roofs appeared in the distance like frozen billows summits of the Pentlaw Hills.

John Tod emerged from the church and looking neither to right nor left hurried across the street – his strut disturbed, his head bowed forward – and disappeared into the shadow of the presbytery house. He had had another of his visions during the Mass, he would be in a bearish humour, thought Uisdean MacUalraig, and reproached himself for the censorious thought. The tall priest hung a moment longer looking where there was a curious effect to westwards – the world, snow-white clad, appearing insubstantial, floating, while all solidity had passed into the heavy, leaden sky.

While he was admiring this rarity he began to think he detected, whether in his ears or as if down by his feet, a tiny, drumming sound. He gave attention to it, trying to pick it up. At once it was unmistakable, and was growing more distinct. Rising, it seemed to swim about him – a continuous drumming sound, regular, though seeming to contain irregularities. Rapidly it drew nearer till, though still small, it drummed on the surrounding air. It stopped, and there seemed to be some shouting – at the North Port,

that could only be. When it recommenced, all at once
much louder, a clinking sound within it brought sudden
completest recognition – it was the sound of horses ridden
at a canter! He felt surprise. To his right not far away
was a corner, and here they suddenly appeared . . . some
ten, twenty, thirty mounted men scattering shattered
moonlight from armour and accoutrements. Even as he
looked at them with astonishment they dropped to a walk
and came slowly towards him along the road, breathing
out their breath in a smoking cloud around them, with
frosty tinkle of bit and bridle, and an increasing creaking
of saddle-leather. When they came abreast he saw with
more astonishment that the horses had been ridden hard.
As they went slowly past – the irregular clip-clop of many
hoofs muffled on the snow-covered ground – the jingling
of metal and creaking of leather seemed loud. The riders
moving with their uncomfortable-looking motion forwards
and backwards in the saddles. One of the horses as it passed repeatedly shaking its bridle and giving vent to a hoarse
coughing. One and another of the grim, bearded men gave
him an impersonal glance above his smoking breath. A
number seemed however to cast what he thought were
looks of some surprise about the street and more than
one as they passed glanced enquiringly up at the steeple.
One turned and addressed an indistinct remark, in which
however the word 'bells' in Scottish seemed to occur, to his
neighbour, and then both gave an enquiring look upward.
A little farther on they bore to the right and began going
down to the south, their noise slowly going along with
them. As they went down the rather steep incline the
hips of the horses were seen rising and falling alternately
at each step, the tails hanging down limply.

They had scarcely gone from sight, and the sound
of their going was still muffled on the air, when away to

northward, from the road by which they had come, rose
– still more unseasonably startling – the wail of pipes. He
opened a wide look before him, wondering what on the
face of the frost-bound earth could be afoot this night.
But hardly had the pipes risen in volume when they died
again; he imagined some interruption breaking in. Again
there was a drumming on the ground, some commotion or
shouting in the direction of the North Port, and he found
himself looking, somewhat startled, towards the corner
where the road turned towards him. On the dull ground
there came a sound of galloping. He waited expectantly,
held by some excitement.

A big horse shot into sight. In the brilliant moonlight
his eye caught the device of the armoured man sitting
on its back and he took a step backwards in amazement
. . . *the Bishop!* If the Bishop noticed him standing there
he gave no sign. As he came abreast he addressed the
horse with a sharp exclamation and touched with his
spurs and the horse went belly-to-earth over the head
of the brae out of sight. Immediately the whole air was
full of galloping when a large body of horsemen rounded
the corner, flashing in the moon, and swept past in a
momentarily stupefying rumble and clatter, making full
speed to overtake their leader. Uisdean MacUalraig,
considerably perturbed, stood gaping at their point of
disappearance.

A man came out of the church: a man with a square
dark beard – the sacristan – and seeing him approached.

"Did I hear horse?" he asked in casual tones.

But before Uisdean MacUalraig had time to reply he
felt his shoulder clutched convulsively.

"God's Blude!" the sacristan was screaming at his
side; and, pointing a shaking hand to southward . . . *"The
beacon!"*

Wheeling about he dashed back into the church.

On the summit of a hill away to southward a point of fire had indeed sprung up. Uisdean MacUalraig was gaping at it in mute incredulity when two sounds shook about him in quick succession and the peace of the night was shattered to the stars. From the north road, inside the gates, the roar of pipes went up into the air. And above his head, from the steeple of the church, rang out a thunderous . . . *boom!*

Before he knew it he was flying into the presbytery house, even as overhead the iron, mile-wide echo was ringingly impacted into soaring fragments by the second 'boom'.

Crying . . . *"John! John! John!"*

Not to be seen!

He dashed to his chamber and stood upon the threshold. John Tod was lying on the floor, on his face, his arms spread out.

"Up, up, John! No time now for prayers!" – shouting, for the bells were ringing madly and the house shaking in the clamour . . . *"The English are ower the border!"*

John Tod came to his feet, looking confused, shaking, his eyes glittering in a chalk-like face. "I am a *priest!*" he shouted back . . . "and no a sodjer!"

Uisdean MacUalraig in the act of turning away shouted back . . . "It's as a priest there's need o ye!" And louder than ever because of the defiant screaming of pipes shrilling past outside . . . "Men deein out yonder!"

He was hardly gone – and now was added the reverberating tramp of men – when he came back. "And put a swoord on ye!" – making exasperated gestures with his hands: the noise was deafening – "They'll spare ye the less for that ye are a priest!"

3

THEIR two figures were crawling across an expanse of elevated plain all white with snow faintly ridged by a wind that was no longer blowing. Not another figure was in sight, not a point of movement anywhere; as if man had been silently subtracted from creation. Leaving only a beacon, glowing ahead, as a sign that he had once been present. Man had gone – and the voice of man! Uisdean MacUalraig had not spoken for what seemed an eternity of years, only sat muffled and remote on his horse, his eyes, fixed on the distance, deep-shadowed under the accentuated line of his strong brows. In an audible silence shone down the moon. Or it was the cold striking against cold in that vast vault that made a lonely music. The eye travelled in all directions to the utmost verge and found nothing more palpable to rest upon than blue translucent shadows lying among the hills. From this boundless emptiness of a glittering world grown feathery as an illusion, shone upon by the cold moon and multitudinous stars, amid silence frozen in immensity, there came forth a measureless indifference, like an emanation creeping chill into the soul.

John Tod shivered, suffering again in the nerve of his sensibility that coldness of objects and things, the hardness of the world's averted face. At some time, long ago, he had strayed into this inhospitable, unfriendly mode, where the rule was strangeness and a sort of unreality, which yet was immovable to the aspiring will and had the power to crush the sense of self. For if one tried to bend that unreality, shot a wish against it, the shaft though feathered with intensity fell limp to earth, and the sole effect accruing was that constriction of the throat and the sensation of vexed tears behind the eyes. One could not budge it, could not turn it towards oneself, the inexorable external, the world of things and men grown indifferent and strange. There remained the chill and smallness. He did not know the path of return to that other, friendly mode . . . For once there had been warmth in the world without, responsive size within himself – would there might be again! Once on a time – he could not have imagined it: the good days! – the external was all a mother, happed him with a mother's hands, was not inexorable but indulgent, smiled on him – on him only – with fond eyes in which he saw himself as of a magnitude and consequence he felt were rightly his, but had since been taken from him. He softened inwardly and was consoled, yielding his secret ear to that recollected voice, warm though so distant . . .

It was Uisdean MacUalraig's voice that brought him to himself, and Uisdean MacUalraig's hand touching his breast. He must have been nodding on the horse, for they had left the high white moor. They were standing on a road or track, with woods around casting jetty shadows. Uisdean was pointing across his breast to something lying at the road's edge. It was a wayside shrine of the rude kind that countrymen put up; to which, passing, they doff their bonnets with a muttered prayer. It had been thrown down and trampled on: there were the marks of many hoofprints all about the place.

"Heretics!" said Uisdean, pointing, and as usual some quality in his voice as always having the power of making all objects sit down firmly on the solid earth. "Tak tent now, John!" he said, and again put his horse in motion.

They left the road and skirted upwards through the trees. Above was the moor again, snow-covered, virgin of hoofprints, and the silence. The beacon larger and nearer, right ahead.

They came to a downward slope, and a red light fell on their faces. A village was smouldering below. At the farther end, lifted up above the village on a knoll, stood a roofless church, glowing red within. They looked at each other, halted; a moment later on with watchfulness, stepping downward through the snow.

About the church the men of the place were lying, in all attitudes, young boys among them and ancient men with grey beards pointing to the sky. In front of them mounds of English dead. Heat throbbed from the stone church, reaching them where they were. Covering their mouths and noses because of the corpses roasting within they sheered away, unable to approach or linger.

Soon they were skirting the base of the hill on whose summit the beacon glowed redly. Here the surface of the track was black and muddy from the recent passage of many feet of men and horses. The south side of the hill proved to be covered with a wood of medium-sized trees growing pretty closely. They had not yet come abreast of the edge of it when John Tod gave an exclamation . . . "Wha's that? Wha's that?" – reining back his horse.

A figure in armour had stepped out from the trees and was standing, full in the moonlight, looking in their direction. Now they could detect, too, that there were horses and men in the wood. The armoured figure came stepping towards them – a very tall man in flashing steel, a sword by his side.

"Wha are ye?" cried John Tod, shifting in his seat, and when the soldier in reply said something in the Scottish language, exclaimed in impatience and turned enquiringly to Uisdean MacUalraig.

The soldier and Uisdean MacUalraig began at once conversing together in Scottish and paid no heed to John Tod, who moved in his saddle, looking first at one and then the other, with a hopeful stretching of his neck as if he would have projected himself between them, and

then, when their attention was not attracted to him, with
an indrawn look like hurt reproach and the creeping on
of an air of discouragement. He turned from them at
last and sat looking out into the cold night, in which
they left him quite alone. He was conscious, hearing his
voice, of Uisdean MacUalraig's mind working with grave
calmness beside him. But most of all he was conscious
of the iron man standing near him, gleaming coldly, an
unknown element of force inside indifferent steel. He
dropped because of that, and was carried away back to
an event in the distant past of his life, never forgotten,
carried within him, indeed, ever since, even when not
present in recollection, insofar as it had marked a change
in the manner in which he was ever after conscious of
himself. He did not like men-at-arms . . .

He must have been very young: the men-at-arms
seemed enormous; but he had no reason not to accept
their appearance as a natural apparition in that world of
moving or stationary objects which he had never yet had
reason to doubt – even if it was in front of his eyes and
not within his mind and feeling – was nevertheless there
because of him, *for* him, depending on him, having him
as its centre and governing point. In any case they were
all laughing as they approached, teeth gleaming white in
every beard; to him it was like a jest he was making
himself: he suffered no disquietude even if they grew
more colossal every instant, crushing the ground under
their feet. They were continuing some jest that had been
going on amongst them when they came tumbling from
the tavern, with jostling and playful smiting of each other.
John Tod was looking on with delight at the scene they
provided for him, answering with all his heart to the
spectacle of power expressing itself in freedom. Just as
they came abreast of him one turned and with a sudden

swing of a mighty arm struck another right on the side of the head (he heard again how the smack from under his open palm burst loud on the air). The other stumbled backward under the unexpected blow and getting the point of his sword between his legs, suddenly, with a loud crash, and sending up the dust, measured his length with hearty goodwill along the ground. Roars of laughter broke forth, all of them looking down with wide-open mouths, some with knees bending weakly, at their comrade lying, heaving with laughter, on the ground. His teeth showed in his beard first as he struggled up to his elbows: his face red, he lay there helpless and neighing while the bellowing of the rest redoubled. He himself, John, was roaring as one of them, feeling himself as powerful as the house against which he had been leaning. And in that consciousness found himself in motion, towards the soldier who had struck the blow, swaying and shuffling in the dust, hands swinging open in readiness to clutch, full of a massive fun. The soldier from watching his comrade pick himself up caught sight of him coming towards him, the rest having already turned about and gone trailing large-legged away along the street. For the first moment the soldier's light-blue eyes when they fell on him continued laughing in his flushed face above his beard. Then their expression sobered. He gave an amazed frown. John Tod was halted, thunderstruck, in his tracks, with an instantaneous premonition, like something acid, cold and flickering in his bowels. The next instant he had turned completely to ice: and standing, and through fascinated eyes, with agonising pain, received death out of the soldier's eyes. An incredible flash of – something he had never known, had never known could be – dislike; cold, immediate, intense. He had looked into a new world not himself – *and there was nothing there for him*. Only that steely, contemptuous flash and

the man-at-arms was already making haste to overtake
his comrades. But John Tod now knew – and was never
to shake off the knowledge – that the 'he' that had been
till now all he was aware of (with the warm, external things
that he had hitherto taken to be an aura of reflection of
himself that he carried about with him), did not make
up the whole: that there was another reality, not–'he',
unimaginably immense, greater, harder, stronger than
himself, which had just taken note of him and for which
– terrible, terrible realisation – he did not matter. And that
he was utterly powerless to make that not-'he' part of him,
had nothing in him capable of turning it towards him or
compelling it to accept and value him. The shock of his first
encounter with the not-'he' had penetrated to the quick of
his being, awakening him, in an instant blindingly bright,
devastating as a thunderbolt, to a new waste state within,
a new 'he' that was always to be 'he', that he was always
to know thereafter as himself, and whose sour, astringent
taste he felt at such a moment as the present was the only
flavour ever yielded to him by his self- awareness. The
former 'he' that he had known and savoured was in an
instant gone, unrecapturable – except that ever since it had
continued to live on, unclear and beyond his grasp, in the
form of a dim longing or reaching out of some desire, ever
frustrated, that was part of his perpetual self- awareness
too, side by side with and mingling with the new 'he' that
had been born that moment.

  Up till that moment he had as it were been playing at
his childhood games *behind the back of* the external-real,
the not-'he', in happy ignorance of its existence – for
the bosom and warm arms, the appraising, 'recognising'
words spoken to him, the friendly face of the objects he
had always known about him, had been like outer parts
of himself: – and then without premonition or warning

that external-real, that not-'he', had turned its face and looked at him, and he at once recognised it for real, for not-himself, for immeasurably strong, for cold and hard, inimical. One glance from its basilisk eye, the seat and fountain of the now for the first time known forces of indifference and dislike, had shrivelled him to a thing of no value and singed the pinions of his hitherto free and playful will . . .

For long afterwards he had the impression that the soldier had struck him, left him rolling in the dust, but he knew it could not have been so, for when he came to himself he was still standing, a mountainous desolation going out of him towards the retreating indifferent back . . . Ever since, the armour of armed men whenever he saw it, especially when it was close to him, brought it all back with fresh force upon his spirit, and chilled in him the sense both of potency and consequence . . .

There had been a postscript. A little priest in a shabby cassock appeared on the street and the swaggering men-at-arms, for whom he was already doubtless non-existent, left their jesting and raised their hands to their bonnets as he passed. In the midst of his new, stupefying realisation the armed monsters appeared within his vision subduing themselves to the little man in a shabby cassock who with a casual wave of the hand in their direction called out a remark that set them laughing again. Seeing this some excitement rose in him, by which he seemed to climb a little out of his desolation.

Something about the boy standing by himself may have struck the priest for when he came opposite him he stopped.

His voice, with a smile in it, said, "And what do they cry ye, mannock?"

"John Tod," he perked up gratefully, looking across

at him – certainly a shabby priest, and how much smaller than the monsters.

"Aye . . . John? And what are ye to be?"

"I am gaean to be . . ." – of a sudden it came to him out of nowhere with completest, final conviction – "a priest!"

4

"WHA is he?"

They had left the armoured man and his soldiers behind and were going forward.

"He is fra Menteith, and his men."

They angled up through the wood in silence.

At length – "But how then are they here afore us?" called John Tod, passing between the trees. "We are weil to the southward of them."

"They were warned afore us," Uisdean MacUalraig called back, steering his own course.

John Tod considered that. "But how could that be?" he called. "How could that be, awa to the north? How could they be warned afore us?"

The wood getting more open the horses came together again. As by a mutual impulse their riders drew them to a halt, almost facing each other.

"John," said Uisdean MacUalraig with a sombre look, heaviness in his voice, "ye maun ken we are but latecomers. That beacon that suld ha' warned us was never lichted . . . till it was lichted by the Menteith men themsels whan they gat here. It may weil be the men of other different pairts are nocht in arms this nicht for that the beacons that suld hae warned them were never lichted . . ."

John Tod gasped as understanding came to him. The other brought himself to continue only with effort. "The

Menteith men fand fower deid men by the beacon, John. Fower that had been to licht it . . . afore others cam upon them that slew them!"

The small, red-haired priest started, glanced this way and that among the trees; whispered ". . . *the traitors!*" They sat looking at each other.

John Tod said, low, "Wha killed the men at the beacon?"

"They had no word but about a man with a long, black beard," said Uisdean MacUalraig.

A sudden sound from right ahead was like a distant, heavy crash. They raised their heads and sat listening. There came a distant sound like far-off shouting.

"Far awa yet," said Uisdean MacUalraig, and clicking his tongue to the horse began to move forward.

At the top of the ridge a man was sitting his horse in the shadow of a clump of trees whose upper arms had been made to grow out sideways by the steady force of winds in those uplands. He turned his head, frowning, and the moonlight showing a tall priest on a grey horse and by his left side a smaller, compact of build and red-haired, on a black, raised his hand to his steel cap and turned away again and resumed his watching.

AT the moment it was like a battle on a tapestry. A vast white ground was dotted over in the distance with small black figures. No sound of conflict came. But ever and again, as though a draught had rippled the stuff faintly, movements here and there could be detected and silver points would sparkle out under the moon. From the ridge where the two priests and the man-at-arms sat in the shadow of the wind-woven branches the ground sloped gently down, to a small watercourse apparently, then

gently up again to a second ridge. Half-way between
the watercourse and the far line of sky, on the long
snow-covered slope, a strong company of Scottish foot
had stood to the encounter. They were drawn up in
a wide, tight circle; its centre, plainly visible to the
watchers, occupied by a motionless group that seemed to
be a small company dismounted from their horses. There
was something menacing and implacable in the absolute
immobility of that circle: it looked animate yet unhuman,
suggesting some gigantic spider squatting on the slope. In
front of it at various points were long black heaps.

The grisly circle still standing in its attitude of waiting
menace, among the English gathered away to the right an
apparently confused movement of milling about started
up. They were forming into ranks: in a very little time
they had shrunk and quietened to a solid object on the
snow. Followed a moment when over the entire field
movement seemed arrested forever. Springing to life the
black etincelating shape launched itself forward, and the
suddenly thin-looking circle of spears seemed even at
that distance to quiver and draw together to receive
the impact. Still they were like painted figures moving
on a painted field, all in a watching silence. But when
the cavalry had covered half the distance there came a
trickling in the ears that was their heavy drumming. The
mass could be seen to meet and shake against the line,
while the drumming still continued. Only a moment later
did it change with a sudden far-off clapping, to become a
tiny clangour wavering in the ears.

But the line held firm. After a time it seemed as if the
mass was not so blackly pressed against the circle's rim.
Then there was no doubt of it, the horsemen were retiring.
White appeared between them and the long black heap
left new before the spears. They drew off slowly, halted,

moved to a new position on the farther slope to southward, halted again: it looked as if they would repeat their charge. But it was the end of the action. After an apparently hesitating moment they wheeled about and rode slowly away up the slope.

The last had scarcely vanished when the ring opened, a group of men mounted on small horses passed through and appeared in the open, and spreading out fan-wise trotted nimbly after towards the distant ridge. Until they reached it the spearmen below maintained formation. Then, some signal having passed no doubt, the ring suddenly crumpled and vanished and in its place was a solid column marching away doggedly in the invaders' wake. Without warning the watching man-at-arms under the trees gave an ear-splitting whistle, answered at once faintly from where the Menteith men were waiting below.

"Forward now, John!" said Uisdean MacUalraig, and they started down the slope.

As they approached the place the impression of a picture faded. Its smell was crude and real; of blood and entrails of men and horses with which the trampled ground was putrid, torn flesh, and sweat and leather. The dark heaps gave forth a sound; horses groaning with a human voice, and a subdued unhuman howling and muted yelping of men. They became shapes: trunks and limbs lying inextricably, many transfixed in violent attitudes. From time to time they heaved in a convulsion, some great horse rolling in its agony, thrashing with its legs; and there would rise a fearful screaming, followed by whimpers or screaming still more fearful, or else by sudden silence as some wounded wretch had his brains kicked out or was crushed under and smothered in the bloody slush.

The Scots had not escaped scatheless either. Inside

the space where the circle had stood there were figures,
some reclining, others motionless on the ground. Uisdean
MacUalraig, suppressing a grimacing shudder of nausea
because of the tepid acridity exhaling from the heaps,
shouted, "Have you need of a priest?" and in Teutonic,
"Do ye need a priest?"

Several figures moved to look at him. One stout fellow
nearby seated against the back of a dead horse, his head-
piece between outspread feet, half-turned and disclosed
his bearded face, the lips stretched in the semblance of a
wide grin or snarl because he was grasping in his strong
teeth the end of a clout that he was binding about his naked
forearm, which he was holding up bent across his front.
Not far beyond him a dark form was kneeling on one knee,
stooping over one who lay extended on his back. Just then
he took the hands of the recumbent one and crossed them
quietly on his breast. His hand rose white in the moonlight
in the sign of the Cross. He got up: a slim man of middle
height.

"Good be to you," his voice came over in casual tones.
"*I* am a priest!"

The brisk jingling party on horses of different colours
riding up were the men from Menteith, their tall captain
on a big black in the lead. Uisdean MacUalraig having
made his acquaintance caused his grey horse to fall in
beside him. John Tod allowed all to pass and fell in at the
rear, as he did so noticing that still another party, whom he
recognised at a glance as mounted pikemen, were coming
up behind, jigging forward at a fast trot.

Shortly the men behind had closed the distance. He
was aware of them riding at his back. He did not look
round, and the whole column rode steadily on together,
trotting, then walking, then trotting again, all in the silent
night.

The leader of the group of mounted pikemen came up behind John Tod. Without any preliminary he began in a matter-of-fact voice speaking from behind his shoulder.

"I had a little daughter. Three years old. Her blue eyes were ever dancing, the golden hair dancing in ringlets round her head, her little feet so light they seemed only to brush this evil earth. Ah, man, a sweet, blithe sprite . . .! Three years she brought light among us. When the English came she laughed and danced to see the torches flaming on their breastplates and their helmets, standing before them in her shift, that scarcely covered her little rosy buttocks. The leader of them held the point of the spear towards her, making some play with it as if it was a jest, and laughing. She even put out her hands . . . such soft, warm little hands she had! And then – would you believe this, sir? – he laughed and plunged it into her body, and still laughing, threw her down against the wall. I saw her there, not long ago. Very tiny she looked. Just a flower crumpled and thrown down beside the wall. Her ringlets in the blood. Quite still. And all so sudden, you know; I couldn't take it in. And her little arms . . . folded on her little bloodied breast . . . I was standing looking at them . . . and all the time I could feel them tightening warm about my neck . . ."

John Tod had understood only the drift of this. When spoken to in Scottish he always felt first a self-conscious irritation, then if he could not escape, a kind of angry impatience not unmingled with contempt, and he had kept his face, marked with exasperation, to the front and even a little turned away; – in any case this was a rather frightening man; he would have been glad if he had taken himself elsewhere, with his story.

But he was struck by the shuddering break in the voice behind him. He looked back across his shoulder. The eyes under the glinting snout of the pikeman's helmet were not on him but looking far in the distance.

John Tod shrank from the close sight of that gentle, dreamy gaze which seemed to him so much more implacable than fury.

5

THEY were in a wood on a short northward slope, out of sight. From time to time in the clear air sounds reached them from the English camp which lay away behind them to southward. On their left, to westward, about a mile away, another body of English cavalry could be seen through the frosted trees debouching, in ever extending procession, from a gap in low hills. From near that gap a ravine whose steep bush-clad sides ran shadowed and black across the country, came curving along the front of the wood, and near the end of it, through a sudden falling of the land, dropped away to a mere bed of a frozen burn, across which the Scots, in their position in the wood, had clear access in front to some miles of level plain. The course of the approaching English would take them past the front of the wood, on the hither side of the ravine.

In the wood the Menteith captain was speaking . . . "Now, lads, the watchword is silence. 'Tis our only hope. To your posts, spearmen on the left, and pray to all your saints they do not sight us or we are nothing but dead men. Let the spearmen keep shoulder to shoulder and thrust with a will; once in the ravine they should be safe enough, for the Englishmen will scarcely dismount; they are glutted for this night and thinking only of the good Scottish beef roasting at this moment in their camp back yonder. To your posts, quickly! And remember – silence, as you hope to see your mothers! Wait for the signal!"

After that there was a stealthy noise that went on for

a little, with twigs crackling and occasional small clinkings. In a succession of places patches of moonlight tilted and flattened, or leapt up and slithered to the ground again over forms moving through the trees.

There were glimpses of spearmen going to the left, then no more; they appeared to have gone stooping with careful steps altogether from the scene. The wood stilled, with diminished cracklings of frozen twigs ever fewer and more furtive. Then it had stilled into apparent emptiness. Only on a close, attentive scrutiny would here and there a part of man or animal be detected, picked out by the moon or marked against the light in front, a shoulder, a part of a face, an unmoving arm or elbow – till it dawned, like a blow, that the silent wood was breathing full.

On the right the horsemen were in a flattened wedge-formation, roughly because of intervening trees. The horses, experienced in the play of war, seemed by their own instinct to merge with the shapes of light and shadow; there they remained immobile, without cough or whinny. Out in front, seen through a black lattice-work of twigs and branches, the snowy level below and beyond the ravine appeared to flicker, in alternate instants blue and glistering. It was awesome, the stillness. John Tod, in his position behind the tip of the wedge, shivered, glancing downwards aside to his left at the blade in Uisdean MacUalraig's right hand, shining blue-dark against the smoky white of the horse's shadowed side. Below, foremost in the wedge, was the Menteith captain. That was his broad shoulder clearly drawn against the white ground out beyond, and the arm to the elbow, the line of the armoured body to the waist, nothing more except the side of his helmeted head. And everything in the wood minute by minute in a rock-like tenseness, a steadied impulsion of mail-clad malice, an implacable wall waiting in the shadows to go down – as it

would go down – in a death-bearing crash. And that man
with the father's outraged heart, *he* was waiting there now,
somewhere in the wood. Recalling the gentle, dreamy look
he had seen in his eyes John Tod shivered, and felt the cold
increase. As if the earth were breathing it outward from
itself, in rhythmic gusts. With each in-drawn breath the
landscape lifted, and in each shuddering subsidence the
trees were shaken farther apart, and the men under them
stood more visible. It got more open all about, and the
cold swept round as if it were a wind. But then with an
agile and adept turning all this became external, only the
surface continued to be freezingly blown upon, he himself
was crawling upwards in haste and eagerness in a short
dark passage. He reached a strait chamber all dark and
warm – he knew it; knew he had been there before –
which his form entirely filled. And curling up, his knees
to his chin, within the soft pressure of its enclosing walls,
felt himself falling over to sleep soothed and secure in the
retired, blood-warm dark . . .

There came a faint jingle, a quiet clopping, muffled
voices heard intermittently, passing along the face of the
wood. After a long time in which the sounds were continuous but appeared to come but little nearer, the farthest of
the spearmen with a faint surprise saw them already passing before the tree trunks. In twos and threes, riding easily
in the secure and unsuspecting sense of nearness to their
camp. More and more of them, moving with short irregular
forward jerks on their walking horses, so many hoofs with
a faint continuous hiss disturbing the snow. Their steel
caps flashed continuously, on breasts and backpieces and
armoured points sparklings were incessant. Ever and again
there were plumes and pennons. The displacement of their
easy passing through the crystal stillness came like a chill
breath among the trees and feather-light touched eyes and

cheekbones. When one of them said something in his own language to his neighbour it was surprisingly distinct, and the short laugh that followed.

On they went, with their leathery creaking: it seemed miraculous that not one so far had turned to look into the wood. Now many had passed along, more and still more were coming – it seemed strange there was no signal.

The first score or so had gone airily past the point where the horsemen were in hiding when from the wood, startling at last even those within it, rang out a clear, bird-like call. Instantly the long line rippled to a halt though at the head, opposite the place where the sound had risen, was prancing and trampling of startled horses. Farther back down the line heads wagged from side to side but in front all were turned in apprehension towards the wood, under whose cover the land seemed, by the noise, to be sliding towards them. Out from the trees, leapt like an apparition a giant with levelled lance on a black horse, and after him and on either hand, at once blurring and reinforcing the impression, others amid a furious bursting of twigs. Even then, while the shocked senses strove to rebut and balance, they received a still more stunning blow, for a cry, weird and strange, rose wavering above the countryside, chilling the blood of those who heard it. The horses at the head of the column danced on the ground; their riders in consternation strove to control them and simultaneously to draw or point their weapons. But gaining impetus at every leap the attackers came like a wind, and before those weapons could be drawn or pointed, and while the echo of that grisly cry still hung in the air, there was a heavy thudding of bodies against bodies, a simultaneous clash and loud outburst of cries of anger and alarm: riders were swept out of their saddles and vanished, horses – seen backing up, pawing

the air – were whirled about and bodily overborne; and
after what had seemed no more than a jar or momentary
checking of their headlong course the ambushers were
through the line, had crossed the burn below the ravine
and were away, opening out across the glittering level with
diminishing four-footed sound.

In their wake some of the wreckage moved; men were
raising themselves on hands and elbows in the trampled
snow, some endeavouring to regain their feet; several
riderless horses had gone cantering a distance after the
Scots as if drawn along in the vortex of their night,
and now they were stopping one by one, looking, with
heads up and ears pointed, after those they had been
following, then wheeling round and trotting on the way
back, but with checkings, haltings to lift their heads, and
bewildered neighings. But on the ground some of the
human wreckage lay quite still, with faces in the snow,
or on their backs with outflung arms, in patches suddenly
and swiftly grown red.

Thus so far everything had gone as hoped and
planned. The score or so English at the head of the
column as soon as they had apprehended the situation,
and having a clear field before them, fled helter-skelter,
energised doubly on the breaking out of that unnatural
cry. Came the clashing impact. Those immediately in
rear of it were thrown backwards or threw themselves
backward upon the ranks behind, and as at the same
time those farther back were pressing forward towards
the point of the disturbances a confused mass was
formed of horses packed together, some endeavouring
to make forward, some to extricate themselves and
retreat to greater safety, many held motionless in the
press. The coolest might shout, 'They are but a few!
Follow!' – but the resulting movement, such as it was,

only made the press closer and more effectively blocked advance.

That was the moment – the column immobilised all down its length – when the spearmen stepped quietly from the trees, and the shouting and agitation were renewed when those halted immediately behind the disordered and congested head of the column perceived themselves menaced close in on their right. This time there was nothing supernatural in their sudden fear; the spears – serpents of moonlight liquid on their venomous tips – were being borne so swiftly in by those grim close-packed men that time was lacking to wheel mounts or level lances. In a moment they had closed, and the heavy flopping attempts at turning gave place to a dancing of maddened horses when they felt the pricks.

The method was to prick the horses whose rearings and plungings unsteadied if they did not quite unseat the riders, many top-heavy in full-mail. Those farthest in advance, pricked in the soft parts of their undefended rear, leapt screaming forward upon the mass now more entangled than ever because trying more desperately to disengage themselves; several were by this alone emptied from their saddles, several more while clinging on precariously, and for the moment helpless, were transfixed and brought clanging down. On the spearmen's opposite or left flank they pricked the horses in the neck or nostrils so that they reared back into and disordered the lines behind, thus holding up for a sufficient moment development of an attack. Simultaneously the same method was being used against those directly in front of the intruding spears. The horses prick-pricked at were bounding and plunging heavily, at every bound approaching nearer the ravine, while their riders rocked about could never steady to point or aim a blow and were severally either struck from their saddles or thrown out of them. Those in full armour, plume and device, came down with a clang that resounded among the excited shouting and lay still and were trampled over by the spearmen's hasty feet. Or else they were still clinging to their saddles when the frantic horses, one after the other, were driven to take to space with a final bound, and dropped, rider and all, into the darkly shadowed ravine, from which then rose the tearing and crashing noise of their descent.

The spearmen with bloodied spears were not an instant standing on the edge before vanishing into the ravine in handfuls and with precipitation. Their clambering noise could be distinctly heard passing backward along the line of the English column: a good number of their horsemen rode their horses to the edge and peered over, inclining themselves forward or sideways. There was a moment of looking about and indecision. But when one horse with a wild screech reared back with blood pouring from its nostrils the movement back was general.

Away over the snow, the party of mounted Menteith men and others were grown small in the distance.

There had been a casualty. The Scot who had been at the extreme right of the wedge of horsemen, being last out of the wood, owing to the prompt flight of the foremost files of English found no one before his weapon. The nearest, however, were still near enough for him to see the shining horseshoes of the hindmost upturned in rapid alternation. Swerving away to his right he set off alone in pursuit. The first he overtook, a man-at-arms galloping all unsuspicious, and taking aim with his lance planted it in his back. The man rose forward off his saddle. First the reins, then his lance dropped from his hands. As his attacker came abreast and swept past he doubled over forward then in a single ponderous but rapidly accelerating movement dived heavily down past the horse's neck. When there came his dry clatter striking the earth the man ahead looked over his shoulder and saw the solitary enemy coming up on his right side, in the act of setting his lance at him transversely over his horse. He gave a startled exclamation and attempted to strike a blow backwards. The hostile point in consequence lodged under his arm and with a screaming cry he dropped his lance and fell forward on his horse's neck. A number of the score or so in front turned their heads, and at that the pursuing man made his horse swerve about and set off to overtake his party.

He had jumped the frozen burn and was stretching out at an accelerating speed across the level when misfortune in a common form overtook him. His horse set its foot in some hole under the snow and came down with such force that he was catapulted into the air. His lance soared and turned above him and landed and stood quivering in the earth after and beyond him. Three, four of those he had been pursuing seeing his plight at once wheeled and made towards him. He was attempting to get to his knees when the first came up and rode him down. Similarly the remaining three one after the other without checking speed rode him into the earth. They checked then, wheeled round and returned. The first to reach him halted, looked down, then, bending forward in his saddle planted his lance-point with deliberation, withdrew it, and with the same deliberation pressed it home again. The other three coming up, all four sat their horses looking down.

The next moment the four of them were looking up, lances erect, heads turned in the direction of the wood and the halted column shining in arms along its front, atop the darkness of the ravine. Shouting had broken out there, an alarmed shouting that was getting louder. And some peculiar movements appeared to be going on in the part of the column behind the entangled mass at its head – violent movements, as if the horses were all jumping up and down together. And the shouting seemed to be centred there. When it was clear that saddles were emptying the four moved off, obliquely, keeping their heads turned in the direction of the disturbance as they moved. The shouting and the dancing up and down of horses in the column grew more and more pronounced. At length some – actually with riders on their backs – were seen to take leave of solid ground altogether and vanish down the dark slope into the ravine. At once the four broke into a hard gallop after their companions in the direction of their camp.

The fallen horse had never moved where it lay bulky in the snow. The lance some distance away stood rigid in the ground at the end of its shadow. A dark patch had grown large round the inert form between. At that moment the man himself was standing in the presence of his Maker, bearing in his hands the merit of his life given freely for a pure good of others, unconsideringly given that the spiritual flower of freedom might adorn his race in the generations to come.

No one had observed his fate. Away in the distance his party slowed and halted, turned to look back, the horses with heaving flanks breathing out their breath like smoke in the frosty air. The long line of English were seen in motion along the front of the wood, then cantering briskly towards their camp and passing out of sight.

"Quite right, my lads!" the Menteith captain apostrophised them softly. "Roast beef is more comforting in the belly than cold steel. We knew *you*!"

Shortly then groups of active dots – the spearmen

– began to be perceived emerging from the head of the ravine and making for the gap to northwards.

"Sweetly!" said the captain softly, sitting easily with his hands crossed above the reins before him.

He turned to Uisdean MacUalraig. In turning his eye fell on John Tod and his smile broadened in his fair beard. With a sideways nod he passed a smiling remark before turning away to look to the duties of his command.

John Tod had noticed. "What did he say?" he said, thrusting forward, "What did he say?"

Uisdean MacUalraig pressed his lips together; his nostrils quivered: he appeared to be in the act of drawing his plaid about his neck with a hitching of his shoulder.

"He says your voice was worth a troop of horse, John."

John Tod winced. His eye followed the captain long and resentfully. Those who came near him were aware of his mood like a bitter patch of bruised blood in the general contentment.

6

LATER in the night they were back near the scene of the ambush. A group that included the Menteith captain and Uisdean MacUalraig were standing by the side of the track recently hoof-beaten by the English, which not far away behind them turned sharply south towards the English camp. The moon was far down in the west. Near them, the ravine loomed jetty black; elsewhere too, shadows were growing all about. The air entering the nostrils was colder than ever. With the hour and the cold a deeper quiet seemed to have descended – seemed rather to be descending. A quiet intense to solidness. One could imagine, looking upwards, boat-shaped concavities of blueness or great translucent petals falling slowly in succession down

the outer blue. In such a quiet the men moved under the
stars, each animating his striding shadow on the lighted
levels.

Those busy in the foreground were carrying stones
in their hands or on their shoulders to the nearby spot
where they were building a cairn above the man who had
been killed. Fifty or sixty yards to northward crouching or
reclining figures were black against the glow of picket fires.
Some two miles farther north a diffused glow hung above
the position of the Scottish army. John Tod had gone there
to find and remain with the men of the burgh.

"Yes, 'tis a weakness in us, Reverence" – the Menteith
captain was speaking of the dead man – "I have seen
a-many such happenings, and actions spoiled and even lost
through it. Yes, I would say that the valiant Scottish men
of our nation are altogether too headlong. Because there
is a flame of manhood in them they fear no advantage in
Saxon bodies, and forget there may be odds even in that
commodity past what is human. Also they think so well
of themselves as men of their weapons – in the which,
par Dieu, they have reason, for there are no better in
the world – that through contempt of enemies they can
be worsted at times by those that fight better by the ruse
and stratagem."

Uisdean MacUalraig smiled, looking about idly in this
lighted and shadowed world. "Have you thought nevertheless that the fault may come in part from this, that we Scots
have always fought only in a just cause, have never tried to
enslave or despoil others, only to defend ourselves. When
your cause is just your eye is single, your heart pure, guile
and cunning do not attract you: the issue is so clear, you
think only of striking a blow for the right, and that as soon
as may be. But this puts you at a disadvantage when you
have to do with men whose intentions are not honourable,

as English intentions towards Scotland have always been dishonourable. For by the very fact that you intend evil towards a man you will be unconsciously disposed to adopt trick and stratagem, rather than meet him face to face whom you intend to wrong. It's a sort of shame of the shameless. If you would strike a man down without cause you would as soon do it from behind: but if in a just cause you would sooner have him before you face to face. That is because the act is purified by the heart's intentions, and conduct without blame follows the desire of righteousness. Whereas evil deeds come with an evil will."

Though the silence was heavy, muting sounds near at hand, yet it could be noticed after a time that it had itself a vague background of noises in the night – far-away noises of uncertain origin that started up and were never completed, dying away with their distant echoes. Uisdean MacUalraig went on . . .

"That would explain the exceedingly fierce hatred the English have for us Scots, who, when all is said, never wronged them nor wished to wrong them. The evil Will darkens the soul with malice towards the person wronged in deed or in intention. So it is that while there is a hatred natural in the one wronged against him who has wronged him, even a great hatred where great wrongs have been done, nonetheless the most violent hatred of all is borne towards the innocent by him that has wronged him or purposes to wrong him. So strange a thing it is, man's heart."

"Strange and ugly if so, Reverence," said the captain. "Certain it is the intentions of the English towards us have always been black indeed, as black as night, and their methods as treacherous as could be devised. No doubt our straighforward Scottish men are badly armed in their singleness of mind against such snakes that strike them from the dark. Think of the Cardinal!"

There was nothing but that curious background of sounds, beyond the stillness. As if an enormous door at an immense distance was standing ajar, and through it one heard the interior cries of a hall vast as the sky . . .

IN the midst of it a particular sound began to stir and come creeping forward till it was half-defined. The faces of the group became overspread with a listening immobility . . . a frowning and straining to locate the increasing sound. Then in the air began a rapid drumming – horses somewhere near had begun to canter . . . Yet none were in sight! As the incredible forced itself upon them they could only look at each other – those horses were approaching from the south, from behind!

Zzzt—the captain's sword came out of its sheath. The sound was now rising like a wave from the beaten ground. "It cannot be!" he muttered, wheeling round. "How could they have passed the scouts?"

There was a flying impression of men getting up by the fires, some even running for horses. The group with the captain stood sword in hand with looks sternly resolved – but even yet incredulous – turned on the elbow of the track. Round which a body of horsemen came fast and right upon them.

The surprise was mutual. The newcomers with a number of half-suppressed shouts pulled up sharply and sat peering forward and down, curious and startled. On the other hand the faces of the Menteith men looking up became overspread with fresh amazement as they slowly dropped their points. There was no mistaking those spare, muscular forms astride the horses, the high-boned, rugged

features and well-spaced eyes . . . Their having passed
the scouts unchallenged was no more a mystery. These
horsemen were Scots.

Their leader was a tall, narrow man in complete
armour. His close-set eyes glinted in the light reflected
from his helmet and curving breastplate. In the first
surprise he had half-drawn his sword, and he retained
his hand on the hilt as he moved his glance from one
to another among the faces below, narrowing his eyes in
a look at once wary and defiant. At length he smiled –
a slow, twisted smile. Slamming the blade back into its
sheath he touched the horse and was in motion again,
smiling his leering smile, casting as he passed a look from
the sides of his narrow eyes.

"What ails yon shamefaced dogs?" said the Menteith
captain as the troop swept up to a canter and went
past, rising and subsiding in the saddles, with faces held
severely to the front or even one might have thought
averted. He caught Uisdean MacUalraig's expression as
he, too, fixedly regarded the retreating backs, and a look
of suspicion came into his frowning face. He swept an
alert, awakened glance after the troop, then back at the
priest beside him.

"Who *is* yon black-faced man, Reverence? Do you
know him?"

Uisdean MacUalraig sighed. "I know him . . . That
is Pitfourie."

"Pitfourie!" The captain scowled. "What is it I have
recently heard about him? Is he not a company-keeper
with the heretics?"

"So it is said."

The soldier narrowed his eyes on the dark mass
retreating, even more indistinct, undulating, with bobbing
heads, along the wood, and his face darkened.

"Traitorous dogs!" he muttered fiercely. "No wonder they were shamefaced. I wonder . . . had they been in the English camp after all? What devil's work have they afoot?"

Uisdean MacUalraig had also at first looked angry, but his expression had now become, rather, thoughtful and sad. When there was a light touch at his elbow and the captain's voice said, low and urgent: "Reverence! The men at the beacon . . . This Pitfourie . . . has he a long black beard?" he replied only with a slow nodding of his head several times, standing very straight and broad-shouldered, his hands clasped one over the other in front of him. By his side the captain also stood looking after the retreating troop, now one dark roundish mass in front of the trees, that went bobbing and shrinking, while its sound from the hard ground decreased in beats out of time with its throbbing rhythm. But his eyes remained narrowed in suspicion and his face fierce and angry.

They saw the mass at last, grown small, the horses apparently no longer cantering but walking, elongate itself sideways to the right and crawl like a many-legged worm over the line and into the thick shadows now shrouding the gap through which the English had come hours before, and in which direction now lay the Scottish camp.

They must have been well through the gap, and the two were about to turn away from watching, when from somewhere in the same direction rose in a distant wail the unexpected sound of pipes.

"What is this now?" the captain exclaimed impatiently, thrusting his hands on his hips and glaring.

Another, longer column appeared from a westerly direction, crawling forward. Before touching the line of shadows it began to alter shape: the head seemed to stop while the rest went on marching, until the tail had marched right into the head and there was nothing but one small roundish mass apparently stationary at the end of the wood –but, as was seen in a moment, containing a pulsing movement. In reality the column had inclined upon its right and was advancing along the front of the trees. The roundish mass swelled, the sound of piping grew louder, beating on the air, coming nearer.

The captain called sharply to two men standing near. "To horse and tell those braggart fools to still their clamour! They will bring a herd of the pudding-bellies down on us!"

The two ran to the nearest horses and mounting galloped away along the wood. After a while the pipes came to a wailing stop. A little later the mounted men returned at a canter.

"Men from Cunningham and Kyle," said the first man swinging his leg over the crupper.

The captain whistled. *"Phe-e-ew!* They have had a march!"

"Since yester even at dusk," said the other man dismounting in his turn.

Slowly, under their eyes, the approaching column grew bulkier. The moon far down towards the hills behind, its light flew restlessly and incessantly about in the forest of slanting pikes, coming low enough to show up by and by blue bonnets by the hundred marching in order; but the faces were shadowed, the bodies a long moving blur. Uisdean MacUalraig was smiling, as if to himself; a thoughtful, kindly smile. Somehow, looking at those foot-weary men approaching, he had seemed to himself to hear far, far away the echo of the eager stir of their departure from their homes some more than twelve hours earlier, in the never-ending quarrel of their country.

At a word the whole company halted some score of paces away and their leader came forward – a slim man of middle height, wearing a sword. He gave the impression of being young; although because of the brilliance of the moon his face was shadowed and somewhat indistinct even when he drew up in front of the foremost of the Menteith group, who were Uisdean MacUalraig and the captain standing side by side, their faces clear in bright direct light. Having given each a sharp glance the newcomer raised his right hand to the edge of his bonnet, then placing his hand across his breast made a short bow to each. Speaking in the broad-vowelled Scottish of the south-west he said: "I have the honour to ask you the whereabouts of the enemy!" As he said it he staggered slightly.

The Menteith captain laughed. "Are you ready for the battle?"

"Ready," replied the newcomer.

The captain laughed even more amusedly . . . "Another of them!"

He turned and pointed with his right hand . . . "The last one of your kind that was here, God rest his foolhardy soul, is lying under that cairn. You want to know where the English are?" – he turned again and pointed with his left in turn – "Just behind that hill. You nearly marched your army straight into their camp, and your pipes squalling."

The other half-turned to follow the direction, disclosing in the light that fell on his face that he was indeed young, with a young, fair beard. He frowned, seeming to try to grasp the situation.

"The Scots are over yonder," went on the captain, pointing again with his right, "on the heights, and the sooner you get your men there the better, for this is not a position for foot-soldiers. We are only an outpost . . . That is, unless you want to sustain the whole battle on your own account if the English should attack."

When the young man having touched his bonnet turned about to give the necessary orders . . . "Hold!" called the Menteith captain . . . "After all, let them rest here!" – with a laugh – "It will not be for long!"

The other had scarce time to give the orders before his men had reached the ground; some sitting, but most in one movement at their full length.

He turned back to say something. But suddenly he swayed towards them. Recovering, he seemed to put up his hand towards the large brooch at his shoulder. But staggered and fell at their feet and began breathing deeply in the snow.

"Here!" called the Menteith captain in a gruff, kindly tone to the two who had done his errand and were standing by. "Wrap the babe in his plaid lest he take a chill!"

The two men stooped over him, smiling in their beards. They undid the brooch, rolled him over, then rolling him back wrapped him in the plaid. His eyelids never stirred.

7

THE moon with an effect of sudden sinking went down behind the hills, and the silver hours were ended. Darkness everywhere rushed skywards, masses of shadow pouring up from the earth into the deep as if to obliterate the stars, which nevertheless presently were shining out more clearly and brightly. In the new-fallen dark the picket fires floated red, while beyond, away to the north, a dull glow suffused in the heavens marked the Scottish camp and the now dying beacon which had blazed as a guide to parties of men hurrying through the night.

By and by there seemed to come a shifting in

the darkness, like its turning on itself. With that a
movement of cold air, as if the earth had stirred in
its frozen sleep. It might have seemed the stars were
paling. Quite suddenly, beyond the darkening east, an
emerald wave of some luminous cold sea tumbled over,
and cast a spume of bitter light along the sky. Therewith
summits and high snow-covered slopes began gleaming
palely all about, creeping from nowhere to hang with a
looming presence in the void. Some were to be caught
sight of far away, brighter-seeming in their smallness and
less mysterious in the recesses of the distance. While this
brightness increased in the upper regions and the sky,
it appeared for a time to intensify the shadows down
below, which lay like a blanket on the levels and thick
and impenetrable between the hills. In this lower darkness
movement became perceptible and a sound began to rise,
and went on swelling: the middle picket fire winked once
or twice, then was shouldered continuously out of sight.
From the direction of the Scottish camp long lines of
cavalry were passing quietly, crossing the burn, continuing
southward along the track through the skirts of the wood.
After them followed, with a different rhythm, their shapes
only just discernible in the diminishing opaque, footmen in
innumerable files. All the time overhead the upper layers
of the darkness were being touched and made mobile and
restlessly evanescent in the constantly descending light, as
the surface of a mist is thinned and driven by the wind, and
the cold, sheeted hills were rising all around more material
and solid. The men of Kyle and Cunningham rose up like
a company of ghosts, and were to be distinguished now
going down to the burn and into the mouth of the ravine:
through the greyness came a series of sharp, splintering
sounds from where they were cracking the ice in order
to mix with water the handful of oatmeal on which they

broke their fast. Reappearing they remounted the bank and stood in order, their forms every instant more solid in the clear-obscure, unmoving, except that – it might have been their pulses passing in so many rhythmic throbs into the shafts which they held upright – above their heads the clearer light, caught on the line of burnished spear-tips like a long filmy scarf entangled, gave forth a certain lambent ripple. All this time the lines of forms were marching across their front, a similar though longer and more marked rhythm of light waving up and down along the spear-points over them. When the last of these had passed the Kyle and Cunningham men moved forward and in a little had gone quietly from the scene.

The company of Menteith men who had been busy with a tightening of girths and overseeing of accoutrements, were now drawn up in readiness: when they mounted, their heads and shoulders rose clear into the growing light. Under that light the features of the frozen face of the world were showing now, rigid and unmysterious.

The captain stopped beside Uisdean MacUalraig, his arms and armour clear and grey-hard as he sat the great black horse. Inclining in the saddle, his face shadowed under the helmet, the spear-head all the while emitting vicious twinklings high above his head.

"Reverence," he said, low, "we shall not all come out of this . . . Remember our poor souls!"

Their hoof-falls were gone on the frozen ground. Just then the sun rimmed the horizon and swept the whole world in a sudden glory of light no less cold though golden. Uisdean MacUalraig raised his hand to order the plaid about him. Having earlier given his horse to replace that of a mounted man he set off forward, crossed the burn, and plodded his way on foot along the track between the trees.

Among whose wintry branches, stark with the morning,
the last tatters of nocturnal shade like belated bats were
taking speedy wing.

8

HE had not yet won through to the other side when a
burst of trumpets rang startlingly out close ahead, with
instantly a somewhat emptied postscript in identical notes
a distance off. Then he was hearing sounds of shouted
commands accompanied by the dry clatter of arms, and
hastened his unsure steps on the icy road.

Beyond, in the open, some five thousand of the Scots
were drawn up in a line of squares, facing south, their
shouldered pikes in a sloping forest leaning towards the
wood behind. Apparently they were just on tiptoe of
advancing. Out in front were the cavalry, not more than
two thousand, drawn out in a thin line which extended
the whole length of the spearmen and beyond on either
flank. The legs of the horses were being wreathed about,
and in a moment had begun to disappear, in an emanation
rising from the white ground, so that a minute later they
appeared to be treading uneasily in a sea whose surface
was breaking belly-high in a froth of swaying foam. Owing
to the line of cavalry and the mist together, nothing could
be made out of the enemy, although their presence was
disclosed by continued urgent trumpetings at no great
distance.

As a matter of fact the advantage both of surprise
and of position lay at that moment with the Scots. The
English, in the arrogance of their superiority in numbers
– which they thought moreover to be greater than it was,
since they had not counted on so large a body of Scots
reaching the assembly point in a single day and night,

especially since beacons were not to have been lighted –
and having, as later appeared, reason to suppose that their
immunity from defeat was otherwise assured as well; had
encamped in a position which placed them now in obvious
jeopardy. For a river with steep banks ran transversely
across their rear and past the right of their line, and if
the advantage went with the Scots in the approaching
onset the English could be pushed over the bank into the
river. Retreat was impossible. Furthermore the arrival of
their outposts to announce the imminent approach of the
Scots had found most of them still feasting or about the
winecups, in relaxation of fancied security – though no
doubt many of the younger and less inured, as well as
some perhaps with lingering human feeling, had sought
therein to obliterate the sights they continued to see
floating before their vision, and dull the sensations they
still felt in hand and arm, of defenceless things that not long
ago had writhed upon their spears. Altogether they were in
meagre heart to face an enemy prepared in sobriety and
resolution, burning with resentment and a sense of wrong.
Battle however they must accept and that instantly: their
opponents were approaching. Throwing forward two or
three thousand bowmen as a screen they hastily drew up
their line – some footmen in the centre in one solid body
and five to six thousand heavily armoured cavalry in two
equal divisions on either side.

Among the Scots a peremptory trumpet sounded:
the embattled squares moved forward. Mist smoked
about their breasts, the helmeted or bonneted heads
rising above it, and the masses of tilted pikes glittering
and flashing high above in the sharp morning light. The
hidden tap and ripple of drums regulated their advance in
rigid line with swift steps. In front the horsemen appeared
to be swimming their mounts in a foaming sea. They went

faster, drawing away ahead, and faster yet, jogged to a trot, lances erect, then at a trumpeted order swept them down to the rest, passing simultaneously at a canter. A moment later one horseman here and there among them swayed top-heavily, or bowed unaccountably forward and disappeared below the rising surface-level of the mist. One horse standing straight up on its hind legs, with pawing hoofs, was left for a moment an isolated object in the view by the breaking of the rest of the line into a charge which carried them at once out of sight behind the greyish curtain. Indeterminate sounds of shouting came, but whether of men triumphing or being vanquished was impossible to determine, blanketed by the mist.

The squares were continuing their rapid march forward, blindly, in an intensely cold, clammy obscurity that had swallowed them with the rising of the mist above the level of their heads. Almost at once however it was possible to see a little way through it and to make out the squares marching abreast on either side: the sun which appeared to have raised the mist was now summarily dispelling it. A pale effect of blueness began to grow overhead against the sky. Dimly made out forms appeared ahead, which rapidly darkened, and became the Scottish cavalry returning. The drums ceased, trumpets rang out again, and in two – for side and rear ranks three – sharp co-ordinated movements the squares had halted, the sides and rear faced outwards, and the masses of pikes were pointed, motionless and firm, against all airts. The cavalry, having discharged their task of scattering the screen of bowmen, came up and cantered past between the squares towards the rear.

So doing they disclosed the whole English line in movement. Coming out of the mist: the horses' hoofs raising a solid wave of broken snow knee-high, above which their heads strained up and down: on their backs

the figures in dull metal sitting, rocking slightly forward
and back, their tossing plumes making a rainbow of
colour against the even curtain of toneless grey behind,
the colours augmented soon by the approaching blazons
and devices – all growing implacably taller and solider and
swifter in their thunderous oncoming, the snow rolling
before them like a billow. The Scots, braced to a rock-like
immobility in a deadly silence, waited in their squares,
presenting an unflickering wall of points. Against these
the English struck with a heavy, splintering crash, and
a cry rose and screaming of horses as they were halted
and made recoil, while with a ghastly bursting out the
colour red sprang to a fluthering predominance over the
lines, and the smell of fresh-torn entrails was suddenly as
solid as if panted forth by the mass of forms straining and
contorting together.

The flanks of the English line, too far extended on
either hand, had been bent forward on the impact and left
hanging in air. It should have been the task of the Scottish
cavalry to charge upon them in that instant of pause while
deprived of their momentum – and they were there for
the purpose, drawn up in two bodies, one on either flank
in the rear of squares of spearmen, facing outwards. The
Menteith captain with his men was near the centre of the
body on the left. Looking round to discover why the
signal was not given to attack the detached and hesitating
portion of the English right, which was before them, and
drive it over the river bank behind, he saw nearby a
helmet opened, and encountered a mocking glance of
two close-set eyes. Eyes which he had seen, unexpectedly
coming upon him, late in the previous night. He felt chilled
as by a premonition. The moment was passing. The enemy
recovered, were reforming their line against them. Still
the signal was not given. Presently the sun, which had

been showing itself like a great yellow disc whirling in the
mist, burst through and sent its cold bright rays flickering
straight into the eyes of the Scots. Then the charge was
sounded – but among the English. They came forward in
a ponderous, straining canter, working up to the gallop,
all lances in rest, when at last the bugle among the Scots
blew the onset. The Menteith men and another company
of about the same number near them with lances pointed
sprang impetuously forward in the endeavour to lessen, as
much as was still possible, the advantage their opponents
now had in both weight of armour and momentum. Then
only they perceived they were alone. The great bulk of
the Scottish horse, on the sounding of the onset, as at
a signal prearranged, had instead of charging wheeled
sharply to the left and were now cantering off the field.
Thus betrayed to their doom the Menteith men and the
others, a hundred against a thousand, charged with a
desperate impetuosity. The impact sent many on both
sides out of their saddles. The remaining Scots, in the
mass of their enemies, made a little agitated swirl which
moved forward, slowed down, was surrounded, moved on
a little, flickered and died.

On the Scottish right flank the stratagem of the cavalry leaders had gone partially astray. A large proportion
of those there, being of a loyalty too notorious, had not
been made privy to the traitorous arrangement. These,
when they saw that the English opposite them were being
allowed to steady themselves and reform, would not wait
the signal. Someone among the centre promptly charged
and brushed off the end of the English line before them,
leaving many mail-clad forms motionless and horses rolling
in the snow. The remaining squadrons blew the onset,
and the right and half the Scots, forming the left and
left-centre, to the number of about five hundred, carrying

out the agreed-on plan, had immediately wheeled right
and set to trotting from the field. The English meantime
had recovered from their surprise at being attacked, and
angered at what they regarded as a piece of treachery,
sounded the charge and bore down upon those horsemen
trotting so nonchalantly across their front. Thus surprised,
a good many of the Scots were emptied from their saddles,
a number put spurs to horse and fled the field, but many
more, angered at what they considered treachery in turn,
or more likely glad to be unbound from the previous
treachery, that of their own leaders, set to engaging
the enemy and giving hearty thrust for thrust and blow
for blow. Meanwhile the loyal five hundred had halted,
wheeled about, reformed, and now crashed at full gallop
into the English rear, and an extremely fierce, confused,
and close-pressed melee ensued upon the spot. This was
the moment at which the sun burst through the dissipating
mist: and shortly thereafter the English from the other
wing, where the horsemen from Menteith and some
others had carried out their hopeless charge, began
streaming over; whereupon the Scots, now in danger of
being overwhelmed with numbers, disengaged themselves
wherever they could. Those whose commanders were not
traitors, the five hundred, retreated towards some broken,
raggedly wooded ground away on the right of the Scottish
line; the others drew away northwards, where they were
awaited by Pitfourie and a thousand more, sitting their
horses observing the progress of things and the effect of
their having quit the field.

All this was a diversion. The main engagement was
going on between the bulk of the English cavalry – and
their foot soldiers, who were now in contact – and the
line of Scottish squares. It was being fought on the part
of the Scots with extraordinary bitterness. The previous

night such as had encountered parties of the English had
fought them doggedly, in the spirit of grim familiar work:
to-day, incited by the vaunting presence and showy force
of the doers of so many outrageous things, every man in
the Scottish ranks nourishing an innumerable resentment,
fought with a tigerish élan, to which the English could only
oppose their sullenness, as it were a weight of resentful
phlegm.

The Scottish lines having failed to break, the English
after a time sounded the retreat and drew away in order to
prepare a second charge. The Scottish spearmen instead of
awaiting them, in their impetuosity vaulted over the heaps
of dead, and reforming instantly, followed on their heels.
This meant the charge had no room to gather impetus
and ended ineffectively, with a loud clattering and the
immediate fall of a number of knights, against the spears.
The lines however were again engaged down their whole
length, with extreme noise and clangour. To the eye they
resembled a band of burnished black, variegated with
colours and scintillatings, drawn across the snow which
the sun, unimpeded now by any shred of mist, was causing
to glitter everywhere – except on the ground of the first
engagement, where there were heaps over which red nets
appeared to have been thrown, rendering them uniformly
dull, and which were giving forth a kind of slow smoke, or
steam. Past these smoking heaps came at speed the English
who had been engaged with the Scottish cavalry, to attack
the squares from the rear, and the contest was fully joined
with great energy on every side.

But with the same lack of effect. In spite of repeated
charges the wall of pikes could not be breached. Moreover
the horsemen were losing heavily, their casualties imped-
ing them more and more. When a spearman fell his place
was instantly taken by the man behind: while the bowmen

shooting from within the squares did fearful execution; against cavalry held at pike point every bolt or arrow finding its mark in horse or man. In the centre the two bodies of foot, Scots and English, had been locked weapon to weapon, like fighting bulls, in an immobility that belied the violent energy being put forth on either side. But the English foot, who were not of the same quality as their cavalry, showed signs of giving ground. Their doing so would have meant the elimination of the entire right wing of English horse, whom the Scottish squares in centre and left wing by swinging round could have enclosed and pressed over the river bank. The danger was obvious: the cavalry of the right wing abruptly discontinued the attack and wheeled away to extricate themselves. At that very moment a large part of the centre gave way, the footmen in fleeing came right in the path of their own cavalry and numbers of their running forms could be seen going down like stuffed men under the horses' surging breasts. The whole English centre and right were thus in loose motion and the corresponding area of the Scottish line pressing forward with cries of "On them! On them!" – while the Scottish right were still held immobile by masses of English cavalry pushing the attack upon it in front, in rear, and on the further flank. Its squares were holding firm – the flags of some burghs were seen standing up steadily like the masts of stranded ships amongst the surf. They must have been glad nonetheless of the partial distractions afforded by the loyal five hundred Scottish horsemen, who had been emerging in a series of sorties from the broken, wooded area in which they had sought shelter and attacking the English from the rear.

The advance of the left and centre had bent the Scottish line forward at an angle; the left now actually resting on the river bank. In front of them the ground was clearing of English, both foot and horse, but for the jetsam of dark, trampled forms scattered here and there. The Scots standing in the squares had at last a respite in which to breathe deeply and freely of the cold air, to wipe their brows, bind up wounds, and stretch their necks to the right to see how it went with their comrades there, whose position could be deduced from the great press of horsemen about them thrusting and smiting at something in their midst, and also by the occasional glimpse of one of their standards disclosed by a movement of the crowded figures. They would then cast their glances up into the clear shallow sky, at the sun not greatly risen above the horizon though already well on its journey across the south, lighting the up-raised cheeks and eyes of those in the front ranks of the squares. The opposite bank of the river was not thirty yards distant from the square farthest to the left. A well-grown wood of hazel clothed its sloping side. Out of the tree tops shot a flock of little birds, out of the wood into the sun, and away down the sky, a swarm of dots at one moment, almost invisible, the next a shower of brazen particles as they swerved like one thing and caught the sun on all the little wings, till at last with a long, steady, sailing descent they checked, flew apart like corn out of a fist, and dropped from sight into another wood dark in the middle distance. The eyes of many men in the squares had followed them in their free flight.

Now that the enemy had all cleared away in front, the voice of the river – a hoarse and profound note – was audible side by side with the noise of the combat on the wing. Then it could be heard that the river had a second voice also, running on above the sullen rumble – an icy hiss.

These two voices sounding together continuously had a note in common, hostile, minatory and implacable.

Except that ever and anon a deep, hollow, pealing tone, a music of rocky underwater chasms, welled up through the heavier voice and sounded out a moment liquid and many-harmonied, when also the hissing voice would break for an instant into iridescent tinklings, before both dropped again to rancour, gnawing and chill.

But something was afoot. Among the English they were sounding the retreat. Those engaged with the right of the Scots broke off and went trailing across the trampled plain; creating a duller impression as they went than when they had first appeared all burnished in the morning. The squares of the right wing were thus disclosed again to view, standing where they had been standing all along behind that screen and press of cavalry. Their fronts noticeably dulled with blood. For some minutes after their opponents had withdrawn to a distance they remained rigid, almost as if inanimate. Then though no man stirred a hairsbreadth from his place life and movement broke out again among them, like a wave passing through the ranks. In a long, slow ripple the bloodied pike heads began rising, reached the perpendicular. The men in the ranks looked about them, with a kind of surprise on seeing again the familiar vista of the white world – a surprise tinged to solemnity, and caused, indeed, by an image still persisting before their wearied senses, of the dancing, kaleidoscopic huddle in front of their spears: an impression of a perpetually tumbling wave filled with horses' teeth and blood-shot nostrils, ears wickedly laid back and straining, sidelong eyes, hoofs rising up and plunging straight down, interspersed with devices on surcoats, and gleaming headpieces, metal men in their saddles lifting their metal arms; all pressing continuously with an inhuman weight, till eye and hand were deadened and another man within one took command and held the shaft like rock endlessly beyond the holding point.

The bearded faces in the front ranks were turned, looking with the same suggestion of stern interest, if not surprise, at the lines of their comrades in the centre squares, and the others farther off, right away to the extreme left standing above the river; and all these in turn looked sternly back, as at those they might never have expected to see again, or whose ordeal, reinforcing the recent recollection of their own, made a solid inward sense of sharp heights of experience surmounted together, if not also still to be traversed with effort even to agony.

For it was never supposed that the English had withdrawn finally. Everyone in fact turned to looking out from the squares, sweeping the ground with their eyes for indications of the tactic in composition. The English had formed in line extending in front of the right wing of the Scots, round their flank and some way along their rear. When they left-turned they formed a column, which then moved forward, its head passing down along the rear of the Scots towards their left wing, while its tail was moving along the front of the Scottish right and round its flank. They went at the slow, walking pace of their horses. Some plumes still made a brave display, with their colours bright against the distant snow-slopes, but many were dishevelled and drooping. The backwards and forwards motion of a man in armour on a moving horse was exaggerated in some cases to a hinted top-heaviness. One man-at-arms on a flecked brown horse turned aside out of the moving column not far along the rear of the squares, and actually came riding slowly toward the Scottish lines; but after a few paces halted. His action had drawn the enquiring notice of a great many of the Scots: those of his own side also as they rode past behind him were turning their heads. He was simply sitting there, with an air of brooding. Those nearest him could now see that the whole of the horse's fore-parts and flanks were being darkly stained. The man changed his brooding air for what appeared to be a great interest in the ground in front of his horse's feet. An intense interest, since it seemed to draw him farther and farther down and forward. As abruptly however he seemed to abandon it for the idea of going to sleep, appearing to rest his cheek against the horse's neck. At the same moment he discarded his lance, which fell to the ground. Meanwhile the foremost of the English had touched the river bank, the whole column halted and faced inwards in a continuous line from end to end in rear of the Scottish squares and round their right flank. The solitary horseman was a conspicuous figure between the two armies: many eyes under iron cowls or through metal slits were regarding him with as narrow an attention as if the fortune of the day hung upon his movements. Thus invested with a nimbus of significance the apparently drowsy horseman gave a portentous nod, and tumbled straight down from the saddle. In the hush that hung about the field the impact of his armoured form upon the armoured ground was distinctly heard, muffled only by the carpet of snow. His foot remained caught in the stirrup, the horse continuing to stand motionless. One of his own side rode forward and tried to disengage the foot from the stirrup with a twist of his inserted lance-point, and failing approached and bending over did it with his hand, and with a tap of his lance set the horse trotting riderless away. After looking down at the prostrate man from the saddle he left him and returned as he had come and wheeling his horse about backed into his place in the line and at once became indistinguishable.

The dead or dying man's horse, as it went, trailed away with it as it were the curtain of curious interest that had for a little clouded the purpose of their being there,

and confronted them again with each other's hostility. The
question was the plan or purpose the English had in mind,
and it was not answered by their having drawn up in line
of attack – for the men they were now facing, in the rear
of the squares, were the freshest in the field, having, with
the exception of those on the right wing, had little to do
all the day: and furthermore in their present position the
English were disadvantaged by having the sun, standing in
the south, striking full in their faces or flickering through
the slits in their visors. To attack from this new position
formed therefore at the most only a part of their plan, as
the Scots were well aware even while their left with a wary
shuffling movement and with lowered pikes drew back
somewhat nearer the English and their right at the same
time moved forward away from them and so straightened
their line. The enemy made no attempt to interfere in these
movements, merely retracing their own left and advancing
their right so as to be still parallel with their opponents.

Now the plan was no longer uncertain. A half-shout
that was also a kind of groan from the Scots front ranks
marked its disclosure . . . *Bowmen!*

These after being scattered at the beginning of the
engagement by the charge of the Scottish cavalry through
the mist, had sought safety behind their own lines. Now
they were seen farther up the river, having emerged from
their place of refuge where they had been reassembled.
At the sight of them coming running forward, a stooping
crowd of figures fitting their arrows to their bowstrings as
they ran, and the numbers of them blackening the snow,
the shout was also like a groan that went up among the
squares and there were bitter maledictions on the traitor
gentry who had deserted with the horse, thus depriving
the footmen of the only effective counter to this species
of attack. Almost all the Scottish bowmen had ere now

become replacements in the ranks of pikemen, but even if still supplied with ammunition they could have been of small avail against such numbers.

The part of the English cavalry was now clear; they were to remain just out of bowshot, too close for the spearmen to risk any rapid evading movement, until the archers at their leisure had thinned out their ranks, when the cavalry would sweep away the remnants in one triumphant charge. Already they visibly animated themselves in prospect of action, a sinister gleam from their arms breaking all down the line.

The bowmen came in to nigh a hundred paces and loosed off a flight which passed like a swift shadow through the air and alighting barbed the ground before the pikemen and caused a movement like a tremor among the men in the front ranks as one here and there fell against his neighbour or sank to earth. Simultaneously however an urgency of trumpets had broken out among the squares, and a second lethal covoy had not quit the wood of lifted bows before the whole line was in motion leftwards; and it had not alighted, causing the same tremor in the ranks, before the square on the extreme left had dropped out of sight over the river bank and its place been taken by the next in order. As the cavalry were close in, constantly feinting as if to charge, the movement had to be carried out with lowered pikes along the rear ranks, slowly, those heart-breaking discharges coming over with a hiss more venomous than that of the river, followed always by the same choked-down cries and men tumbling among their fellows.

For the front ranks a momentarily uplifting sight was the remaining Scottish cavalry, looking few though all the more intrepid in the sweep of white landscape, stretching out from their wooded and broken cover away to the right, in a determined attempt to reach the bowmen and throw confusion in their ranks . They could not possibly have succeeded, however; from the English right wing a much heavier body of horse detached themselves, leaving the spearmen for the present, and went hammering away to intercept them; and some kind of hand-to-hand engagement was seen to be in progress at a considerable distance from the archers. The deadly showers therefore continued to deplete the ranks, and the squares notwithstanding to move with a steady, regular motion leftwards. Two more of them in succession reached the brink and breaking up into their component individuals disappeared over into temporary safety: then the section of cavalry nearest to the river charged the square presently a-top the bank. Their object was by pinning down those nearest the bank to hold up the entire line, on the rest of which the archers might continue to shower their deadly shafts. But only those squares halted which were actually attacked, the rest by inclining forward could pass behind them, and the leftwards movement continued. They were able to move but slowly, however, despite the terrible anxiety to quit the spot, because of the enemy hanging close in and threatening every moment to come down on them. So step by step the wall of spears grew thinner; as they moved they left a trail of men scattered on the ground.

A wind sprang up in the clear north-east, blowing strongly through the empty heavens: those down below on earth felt its movement. Felt it flutter and sway. With a sustained, long hollow pipe or hoot wavering away into the south-west the wind steadied and in one mass the whole space of air moved forward solidly. At that the snow floor stirred and lifted. Its surface was weaved over by broad, fluthering lines. Where two or three of these met in their darting courses the winnowed snow flew up in a powdery column. Behind such a column a section of the bowmen, or a group of horsemen fighting at a distance, would suddenly become grey and indistinct, even for a moment invisible; and then immediately dark and solid and in place again as the tower as quickly toppled or collapsed from sight, or became a madly contorting spiral that rushed vanishing away.

Above the line of the river bank the heads of pikes could be seen moving along in procession: those who had disengaged themselves were making their way upstream to a ford some fifty paces distant. Linked together, they were crossing this thigh deep in rapid water, and climbing up among the tree trunks on the further bank. In this way more than half had crossed or were crossing when from the bank where the remainder were still combatant desperate cries and exultant shouts went up. The bowmen had ceased upon a signal to send their arrows over, and the right wing, the most exhausted in the earlier part of the battle and the most depleted by the arrows, were attacked front, rear and further flank by the full weight of cavalry and were in danger of breaking. "Back! back!" sharply echoed the cries among the trees: the cries in the river – "Back! back!" – were liquified and carried away downwards, becoming hoarsened in the moment of mingling with the note of the water. All turned about and began pressing across the river.

The cries among the clashing forms on the opposite bank grew ever more desperate, ever more exultant. Among the leafless trees on the wooded further bank John Tod was standing, his face blue and drawn with the agony of fatigue, shivering in violent spasms inside drenched clothes turning to ice as high as his waist: his fascinated eyes held on the imminent disaster. A man passing overheard his involuntary and probably unconscious exclamation. He stopped.

"What! Maister Tod! Wad ye hae us gie in to the English?" – shouting above the noise of the conflict and the river – "That's to speak like a heretic!"

The face the man had turned was startling, the shouting mouth a kind of cavern in moustaches and beard of solid white ice from the freezing of the breath he had but now been panting forth in the extremity of exertion, his eyes, deep-sunken in the head, burning with the fever of fatigue.

"Forbye the Suddrons will ne'er be hauden til a bargain," he shouted, his eyes staring solemnly under twin ice-curtains of eyebrows. "Drive the life out of sic vermin, say I; they're no to lippen til abune the earth!"

The shouts rising still louder on the other bank he recollected himself and turning his ice-encumbered face went off quickly, managing his pike among the trees.

Not far away Uisdean MacUalraig was standing, his hands pressed together while his lips moved soundlessly; his eyes fixed on those thin lines of spears on the other bank which could be seen through the trellis of branches, as if to work a miracle by their intensity.

A solid splashing was rising from the river as they crossed in a manful column linked together. Then the splashing suddenly dropped away and down there also shouting started, and among the crowd waiting to enter. There was a second of only the river's voice, then the shouts recommenced, and the splashing in a less solid way, suggesting agitation or disorderly haste. Arrows had begun falling among them. Bowmen had appeared thick on the bank upstream. Now it seemed that all was over: the right were held and being slowly pounded by the English cavalry, the left and centre could not reach them for the arrows in the ford.

But as suddenly the arrows ceased. It was the archers' turn to break out into crying and shouting. Beyond them had risen up a cloud of snow, and against its grey mass the bowmen were seen as dark forms leaping this way and that, all their heads rigidly turned in the direction away from the river and the men in it. Strange noises like animal roaring came intermingled with their shouts, and all at once large shapes – non-human shapes – were seen, cloudily, plunging about among their darting forms in a denser cloud of snow, and louder cries were rising. It was the resource of the indefatigable remnant of Scottish cavalry that had been equal after all to stopping that fatal archery. Frustrated in their attempt to reach the bowmen across the open they had made a wide detour and re-approached unseen from the south-west. Rushing the English camp they had thrown down some stockades penning stolen cattle and stampeded them in the direction of the river, following them right in among the bowmen, who were instantly converted into a panic-stricken mob.

The spearmen in the ford were quick to avail themselves of their immunity. The iron line was again uncoiling from the trees and measuring the breadth of the river with surging tread, pikes bristling above. But their pace increased still more, with a sudden, forward impulse, when changed cries from the bank told of a break in the tension of things and a falling of fortune against their own side. The square on the extreme right, the most borne upon all the day, had in fact at last presented too thin a line of spears against the horses' armoured breasts. These had burst their way inside at first one then several points, and that cry of the English had gone up that meant 'the kill'. A single moment and they were in the centre of the square, and it was broken up into isolated, still resisting fragments. The flag, which had remained erect all day, rocked about as if shaken by a tempest: fell, appeared once again over the heads of the smiting and exulting horsemen and then sank forever. The groups were soon reduced. Any horrified eye in the squares that remained intact could have caught sight only of isolated pikemen still erect in the melee, and those, cloaked in their own life's blood, making some last blind staggering lunges while their enemies struck them at their will until they kneed the ground and fell their length, and perhaps knew for a little the flowing out of their life and the lessening smart of indifferent hoofs spurning their clay.

The spearmen out of the river were running to place their shafts together, and the enemy, not to be caught between two walls of points, broke off their somewhat nagging efforts and retired at a wearied canter, which promptly became a walk. Their seated backs were seen in long lines above drooping tails which the wind bent away sideways. Over their helmeted heads the pennons though heavy with blood snapped like scorpions in the crying wind, even at moments stood straight out from the rippling lance-shafts in their upright rows. The snow smoking from every hoof. The spearmen threw forward a semi-circle of the fresher men of the left-wing who had returned across the river and behind these the fragments of the depleted right made their best haste from the field and down the bank. But although the English halted, wheeled, reformed, and even came some way forward – the bright, low sun evoked few sparklings on their armour now – they contented themselves with hanging menacingly close in, giving those on the bank no occasion but to retire below it as soon as that could in orderly wise be done.

In the shouting ford they were still contending against troubles. Only four or five could cross abreast; moreover they were hampered by wounded men who were being assisted or carried forward; worse, a number of bow-men had restationed themselves on the bank above. To increase confusion some hundred horsemen arrived upon the scene. All that remained of the loyal five hundred of the right wing, they appeared from nowhere, covered with blood. In their midst was the Bishop. His helmet dented, his face like chalk, his eyes filmed and unseeing, he was all but lying on the horse's neck, while from the point of his sword, which still hung from his hand, his blood dripped slowly down. In this state he was led across, followed by his grey-faced, blood-splashed crew, conspicuous at straggling intervals amongst the pikemen who themselves were no less hollow-eyed, and might by their appearance, some of them, have been wallowing overhead in blood.

Of five thousand spears that had begun the day scarce four were making the passage through the river. Every now and then one, either pierced by an arrow or weakened by his wounds, fell, slipped from his comrades' frozen clutch and was instantly swept from sight into deep water. The others went on. The cloud-mass that unnoticed had been racing down the whole sky lipped across the sun and there fell everywhere a greyness, and with it a feeling of more cold. Like capfuls of white feathers snowflakes came to meet them down the shrilling wind. Through the malevolent voice of the river, deep and hoarse, their splashing rose with urgent iciness . . . At last their hasty legs were brushing the snow in ferny hollows of the wood.

After them came the voice of the abandoned field. Many of them, recalling the dishonoured cause of their misfortunes, stood still in the falling snow.

But the field held later and other voices. Voices of gruff command, clinkings of arms, hoof-beats and footfalls, all the opaque grey-pallid snow-filled night . . . following, ever- following south. Christ in the will, the blow befallen earlier was nothing . . . not even a feather.

ANE TRYALL OF HERETIKS

MOVE UP, JOHN
3

PART THREE

I T WAS GREY DAY OUTSIDE. In the chapter-
house the light was little stained, lying in faint
commingling shades across the flagged floor and
over carved stone walls. The clergy in their black – in
a row of stone seats at the end near the door giving
access to the church – were almost natural-complexioned.
But the Bishop's large face in the centre, still pallid from
wounds received in a recent English invasion, appeared
even more sickly because of the tinge thrown over it by
his purple cassock and birettum. Shadowed pouches lay
under his eyes: his air was weary and somewhat absent.
He was reclining his bulky form sideways in his seat, an
elbow resting on one stone arm while he tapped with his
fingers on the other.

On his right hand, nearer the door into the church, a
slender thin-nosed canon with an acid-precise expression
was bending his head aside towards a red-faced, square
built canon who sat next to him, whispering and nodding
his head, holding some papers at which both were looking.
On the Bishop's left hand an aged canon with silver hair,
an air more dreamy and absent than the Bishop's own,
sat looking straight in front of him with a gentle, rather

senile smile on his almost too refined, aristocratic face.
His abstraction and his slender height, the quiet hands
folded before him, contrasted strongly with the air and
person of the canon next on his left. This was a smallish,
ruddy, fair-skinned man whose features and whole presence denoted alertness and a scarce-suppressed vivacity.
With jet black hair and lively eyes, he seemed young to be
a canon. He had just been speaking, making expressive
movements of his hands, to the last canon in the row, on
his left again, a rather pale-faced though robust looking
man whose greying hair had not long since been fiery. He
now turned his mobile dark eyes on the Bishop who at the
same instant stirred, drew himself upright, and casting a
glance about on either side, sighed. Looking across to
someone beyond the open door he called out in a strong
voice with a peremptory accent – "Let them come in!" He
sighed again. A frown passed across his face.

They came in quietly and, at a sign from the Bishop,
went and sat down on a form at some distance from the
clerics, facing them. Two of them. One of the middle
height, dark-haired, sallow and hollow-eyed, in the dress
of a tradesman: the other a short, thick-set, broad-faced
man wearing a soiled friar's habit, but with the friar's girdle
of cord with its pendant knots signifying poverty, chastity
and obedience replaced by a broad leather belt. The
air of both was somewhat strange in the circumstances:
they seemed in some way withdrawn, remote from their
surroundings. The dark man in the tradesman's dress let
his hollow eyes wander over the fretted walls and vaulted
roof, though with no appearance of interest, and along
the bench of ecclesiastics, but without seeming to take
particular heed of them: the stout friar crossed one knee
over the other and taking his chin in the stubby fingers
of his hand – the beard he was growing was an inch long

all round his face – rested his eyes on the ground as if meditating. There appeared to be nothing self-conscious or assumed in this – at any rate on the part of the tradesman. They seemed in some way actually 'unreached' by their situation.

The clerics, on the other hand, were looking at them with interest, the Bishop leaning forward, narrowing his pouched eyes. Failing apparently to penetrate to their state, and coming back to the occasion, he sat up, coughed once behind his hand, and taking a paper which the acid-precise canon on his right held out to him, let his eyes travel over it. Then he raised his head and bending a severe look on the two men before him, pronounced:

"Alexander Cock, baxter, and Robert Coltart, of the Order of the Friars Pauperites, ye are here compeared afore me and divers of the Chapter of this Diocese to be examinit anent certain heresies said to have been utterit and disseminated by you, and to thole the law an ye be guilty. Wherefore as the crime whereof ye are accused is capital, that is, of the heid, and accordant to the law of this Realm to be punishit with death, ye are bidden look weil unto yourselves and to answer in truth and verity all things charged against you, as men whase lives lie at the disposal of their judges."

The two were looking at him while he spoke, but still with some impersonality – they might scarcely have realised his purport.

"And firstly . . . " The Bishop lowered his eyes to the paper in his hands . . . "Firstly, Alexander Cock, these words:" – reading – *"God ordains some to everlasting life, others to everlasting punishment. God does not choose the Elect for ony guid He sees in them, or whilk he sees that they will do; nor does He select some for eternal reprobation because of their ill deeds foreseen by Him. It is impossible to assign ony reason for God's bestowing mercy on His people but just that it pleases Him: and neither has He ony reason for reprobating others but His will."*

He sat frowning. "That's damnable doctrine!" he could be heard to say.

He raised his eyes – "Can ye truly hae said sic a thing, Cock?"

The dark man on whose face a smile of purest pleasure had appeared when he heard the doctrine read out by the Bishop, sprang up at once. In an instant extraordinarily changed. A flush suffused his brow; his sunken eyes shot fire.

"I said it!" he shouted in a defiant, exalted voice, "and the Word o God said it afore me, and now *ye* hae said it, my lord Bishop, and blessed be God that I hae lived to hear a Prince of the Kingdom of Darkness proclaim the truth of God!"

He sat down. The friar beside him cried – "*Consentio!*" A silence fell.

"But, man, this . . . 'tis a grossness." It was the rumbling bass of the square, red-faced canon nearest the door, on the Bishop's extreme right, protesting. He had heavy, overhanging eyebrows and looking forth under them rumbled: "An what ye say were true, Cock, it would mean that God has sent at ony rate some *guid* men to Hell and appointed some ill anes to Heaven. That maks God the doer of injustice – and that is impossible, since Justice is His Nature."

"Wha are ye . . . " – the baker was incensed again, and sprang up, pointing in accusation – "wha are *ye* that daurs limit God in His ain world? God is no to bind wi your *sequitoories* and your *sillyjimmies*! God's will is *free*" – he threw his hands above his head – "free and abune aa!"

"*Nay!* Nay to that, Cock, as ye maintain it." The

lively, young-looking canon had been restless in his seat, his eyes leaping from one person to another as they spoke in turn. Now he could no longer keep silent. "Ae thing God is no free to do," he cried over to the heretics, "and that is to deny His ain Nature. What is mair, could God do injustice here and now, Cock, ye would never ken it; for we and you and this braw kirk and the haill world and the universe entire would instantly dissolve into that naethingness out of the whilk God cried them into being . . . For God created and sustains the universe by His Power, and God's Power *is* God's Justice. For God is Ane –*Ane*, mark that, Cock!; ane absolutely single Being, indivisible, withouten pairts or accidents – His Power is His Justice and His Justice is His Truth and His Truth is His Luve and His Luve is His Power again, and sae through aa His attributes, as we presume to caa them; and ilk ane o these is God Himsel; God's Justice is God Himsel, God's Power is God Himsel, and sae forrit. Because God is *Ane*." His tone and gestures were those of someone who would persuade another by patient exposition; the silver head of the canon by his side nodding the while affirmatively. "Therefore did He deny His Justice, whereby He rules creation, God would also by the same act and of necessity forswear His Power, whereby He made it and sustains it; with the instant consequent of universal dissolution and evanishment. And sae the solid world stands visible in your disproof, since it testifees against ye that God is still a God of Justice in that it witnesses that He is still a God of Power. And ye yoursel refute your ain thesis in the act of stating it, since nane but a just God could hae power to sustain ye in being, able to speak heresy. And sae ye see, Cock, that ye refute your doctrine in your ain person, for an what ye say were true ye couldna be here to say it, nor we to hear it."

The friar who had been smiling superiorly in his ball of beard, shrugged, smiling more widely. The baker after giving his attention for a while, knitting his brows as if trying to understand, had folded his arms and wrapped himself away. He now said nasally, swaying his head: "Think not to confound the Elect of God with philosophy and vain jangling."

The Bishop gave an impatient exclamation. "Ye're the ane to ken about jangling. I houp ye'll no come to ken about hanging!"

"Wha is he that sall condemn?" the baker shouted in declamatory tones, springing up, *"It is Christ Jesus that died"* – he hesitated a moment in mid course as if taken aback, glancing in inquiry as all the clergy at the mention of the Divine Name uncovered their heads, then with an impatient shrug went on – *"Yea, that is risen also again, wha also maketh intercession for us!"*

Silence fell again.

"Nae doubt but ye can cite Scripture, Cock," said the Bishop at last. "But ye'll mind even Satan did that afore ye."

"Wha suld ken it better nor yoursel, my lord, since ye are his servant and he is your Maister!"

The Bishop compressed his lips, reddening. "Cock," he said, controlling his voice, "I sair misdoubt ye for a contumacious heretic. Natheless I will condemn no man till it be certain he is no in error for want of hearing sound doctrine." He looked all about, saying aside: "Wha was deputit theologian?"

Uisdean MacUalraig had been seated by himself against the wall, on the side opposite the door, that is, to the Bishop's left, and between the clerics and the heretics. He got up and bowed, looking towards the Bishop. Just as he rose the sun came through the clouds, for suddenly like a silent acclamation the whole building floated warm with rainbow hues within, so that as the Bishop leant forward peering towards him crimson and purple changed across his face.

"Oh, it's you, is it, Uisdean?" – sitting back again and looking forth at the heretics now stained in the multicoloured radiance whether they would or not – "There's a mislearit knave here has said God decrees the eternal death of them that perish, and that no for ony ill that they may do. Let him hear true doctrine, if sae be he may retract his blasphemy." He clasped his hands above his stomach and with a wearied look prepared to listen.

Uisdean MacUalraig bowed. "My lord," he said in his mild voice, "it could easily be shown from mony texts of the Scriptures and the Fathers that God desireth the salvation of all that believe in Christ. As, however, the less is contained in the greater, it will suffice to show that God wills the salvation of all mankind whomsoever. Now St Paul saith in his Epistle to Timothy: *I desire therefore, first of all, that supplications, prayers, intercessions, and thanksgivings be made for all men. For this is guid and acceptable in the sight of God our Saviour, wha will have all men to be saved, and to come to the knowledge of the truth.*" He turned towards the heretics, saying: "The Apostle commandeth us to pray 'for all men' because this is 'guid and acceptable in the sight of God'. Wherefore is it guid and acceptable? Because 'God will have all men to be saved and to come to the knowledge of the truth'. In other words, God's will to save is universal." He turned towards the Bishop again: "The passage gangs on: *For there is ane God, and ane mediator of God and men, the man Christ Jesus*" – in a ripple of rising hands the clergy uncovered – "*wha gave Himself a ransom for all.*" Turning towards the heretics he repeated: "There is one mediator of God and men, the man Christ Jesus. What doth this signifee? Plainly that the human nature which Christ assumed in the Incarnation is common to all men. Hence, wha ever is a man, has Christ for his mediator."

THE heretics continued sitting side by side looking at him from the sides of their eyes. He therefore went on, speaking into the glowing building: "The Fathers and writers, my lord, are of ane accord in agreement. St Ambrose declares that God willeth to save all men: *He willed all to be His ain whom He establishit and creatit. O man, do not flee and hide thyself! He wants e'en those that flee, and doth not will that those in hiding suld perish.* St Gregory of Nazianzus haulds God's *voluntas salvifica* to be co-extensive in scope with original sin and the atonement: *The law, the prophets, and the sufferings of Christ, by the whilk we were redeemed, are common property and admit of nane exception; but as all are participators in the same Adam, deceivit by the serpent, and subject to death per consequent of sin, sae by the heavenly Adam all are restorit to salvation and by the wood of ignominy recallit to the wood of life, from the whilk we had fallen.* St. Prosper concludeth that, since all men are bounden in duty to pray for their fellow-men, God must needs be willing to save all without exception: *We maun sincerely believe that God willeth all men to be saved, since the Apostle solicitously prescribeth supplication to be made for all.* The question why mony perish St. Prosper answers thus: *God willeth all to be saved to come to the knowledge of the truth, therefore those that are saved, are saved because He wills them to be saved, while those that perish, perish because they deserve to perish.*"

He sat down.

The Bishop was reclining in his chair, tapping the arms softly with his stout fingers, while he regarded the heretics shrewdly, his lips pouted and one eyebrow raised.

"Weil, Cock, " he said, "that wad seem to answer ye. What will ye say now?"

The baker sprang up, instantly transfigured again.

"I say wi the Word of God!" he shouted. Propelled by his energetic breath the rising motes went sailing through the colours in front of him and ascended towards the roof.

Raising his hand he shouted in a reciting voice: "*For this is the word of promise: At this time will I come, and Sara sall have a son. And not only she, but when Rebecca had conceived of our father Isaac*" – he pointed at Uisdean MacUalraig who had resumed his seat, but the pointing was quite impersonal: without knowing why Uisdean MacUalraig seemed at that moment to perceive something essentially simple and as it were personally inoffensive in the cast of the man's nature, along with whatever else was in it – "*For when the bairns were not yet born,*" he went on, "*nor had done ony guid or evil, that the purpose of God, according to election, might stand*" – he jabbed into the air – "*not of works, but of him that calleth, it was said to her: the elder sall serve the younger. As it is written: Jacob have I luvit, but Esau have I hated.*" He sat down, crossed his legs, threw his head on one side, and looked at Uisdean MacUalraig sideways under his lids.

"An it please you, my lord," said Uisdean MacUalraig rising, "this is from the ninth chapter of St Paul's Epistle to the Romans, whilk is the main reliance of them that hauld God absolutely predestinates some to guid and others to evil. The passage quoted is alleged to prove the absolute predestination of Jacob and the negative reprobation of

Esau. But mony theologians have held that Esau was
saved. And forbye" – he turned to the heretics – "the
Apostle speaks not here of predestination to glory, but of
Jacob's vocation to be the progenitor of the Messias. Esau,
wha was not an Israelite but an Idumaean, was simply
passit ower. The passage maun be interpret conform to
the context, that is to say, as referring to the gratuity of
grace, and nocht to predestination."

The baker had not altered his attitude as Uisdean
MacUalraig proceeded, except after a little to take the
end of this thin beard in the tips of his fingers and assume
a mocking or superior expression. He got up. Extending
his finger towards Uisdean MacUalraig unhurriedly, fixing
him with his hollow glance, he recited: "*For He saith to
Moses: I will have mercy on whom I will have mercy, and
I will have compassion on whom I will have compassion*"
– again he took fire – "*So then it is not of him that willeth,
nor of him that runneth, but of God that showeth mercy.
For the Scripture saith to Pharao: To this purpose have I
raised thee, that I may shew my power in thee, and that
my name may be declarit throughout all the earth.*" He
jabbed the air in rhythmic emphasis – "*Therefore he hath
mercy on WHOM he WILL, and WHOM he WILL he
HARDENETH!*" He sat down supremely satisfied and
turning his head aside appeared to smile in his dark brown
beard.

Uisdean MacUalraig rose. "My lord, the same may be
said of this passage, which is from the same chapter. Some
passages of the Scriptures would seem to imply that God
withdraws His grace from them that are obdurate, nay,
that He Himself hardeneth their hearts in punishment
of sin. Thus the Lord saith of Pharao in the Buik of the
Exodus: *I sall harden his heart*; and Moses tells us: *The
Lord hardened Pharao's heart, and he harkened not unto*

them. But it would be wrang to assume that this denotes ane positive action on the part of God. Pharao, as we are tauld in the same Buik, *hardened his ain heart*. The faut in ilk instance lies with the sinner, wha obstinately resists the call of grace. The Fathers speak of God's way of dealing with obdurate sinners in a manner whilk clearly shows their belief that He never entirely withdraws His mercy. They insist that the light of grace is never extinguishit in the present life. *God gave them ower to reprobate mind*, says St Augustine, *for sic is the blindness of the mind. Whasoever is gien ower thereunto is shut out from the inward licht of God, but not wholly as yet, whilst he is in this life. For there is 'outer darkness', whilk is understandit to belong rather to the day of judgment; that he suld rather be wholly without God, whosoever, whilst there is time, refuseth correction.*

"The theological argument, my lord, is weil stated by St Thomas. He distinguishes atween *obstinatio perfecta* and *obstinatio imperfecta* and saith: *Perfect obstinacy exists only in Hell. Imperfect obstinacy is that of a sinner wha has his will sae firmly set on evil that he is incapable of ony but the faintest impulses towards virtue, though e'en these are sufficient to prepare the way for grace.* Again, according to the declaration of the Fourth Lateran Council: *If ony faa into sin after having receivit Baptism, he can be restorit by sincere penance.*"

He turned to the heretics. "Justly, therefore, does the Kirk regard despair of God's mercy as ane additional grievous sin. Whereas if they were richt wha assert that God in the end absolutely abandons the sinner, still mair that He predestines him to perish, there could be nane hope of forgiveness, and despair would be justifeed."

"*O man, wha art thou that repliest against God?*" The baker was up again, arms akimbo, his head held high. Now he had a prophetic or inspired air, as if he was merely a trumpet blown by some power that was not himself, potent though invisible . . . "*Wha art thou that repliest against God? Sall the thing formit say to him that formed it: Why hast thou made me thus? Or hath not the potter power ower the clay, of the same lump to mak ane vessel unto honour, another unto dishonour?*" He spread his hands on his buttocks and thrust his cheek forward – "*What if God, willant to shew his wrath, and to mak known his power, endurit with meikle patience vessels of wrath, fitted for destruction*" – standing erect and throwing out his chest – "*That he micht shew the riches of his glory on the vessels of mercy, whilk he hath preparit unto glory?*" – throwing out his arms in a wide welcoming gesture and with head thrown back and half-closing eyes seeming to inhale deeply, the friar also beside him appearing to sniff the perfume – "*Even US . . . wham also he callit not only of the Jews, but also of the Gentiles.*" He stood for a moment, then sat down and cast a challenging triumphant glance sideways at Uisdean MacUalraig.

The latter got up. "This is from the same chapter, my lord, and is their strongest text. Here the Apostle really seems to hae thought of predestination." (The friar: "Atweil does he!") "But the figure maun-na be pressed beyond what it will bear, lest we arrive at the heretical blasphemy that God positively predestined some men to heaven and others to hell. The *tertium comparationis* is nocht the act of the Divine Artificer, but the willantness of man to yield his will to God like clay in the hands of the potter." He turned to the heretics – "Nor is it admissable to read intil the Apostle's thought even a negative reprobation of certain men. For the primary intention of the Epistle to the Romans is to insist on the gratuity of man's vocation to Christianity and to reject the presumption that the Mosaic law and their bodily descent from Abraham gave the Jews preference ower the heathens. In short, the Epistle to the Romans has no bearing whatever on the speculative question whether or no the free vocation of grace is a necessary result of eternal predestination."

He was heard out impassively, the two looking from the sides of their eyes. But a flush could be seen deepening on the brow of the baker, his nostrils were twitching, and the priest had no sooner finished than he sprang up . . .

"I am nocht hauden to the Romans, as ye appear to think. I stand upon the haill Word of God. Tak this out of the Ephesians – an ye hae read it ye will ken it again when ye hear it – *Accordant as he hath chosen us in Christ afore the foundation of the world. Wha hath predestined us unto the adoption of children through Jesus Christ*" – the clergy uncovered: the movement caught his eye and again he glanced aside at them impatiently – "*unto himsel, accordant to the purpose of his will. In whom also we are called by lot, being predestinated according to the purpose of him wha worketh all things accordant to the counsel of his ain will.* I am but an unlearit man, Messer Theologian, as my lord Bishop hath said, but to me 'all things' signifieth 'all things'. And so He also sends the damned to Hell, since He '*worketh all things accordant to the counsel of His ain will*'."

The friar rasped forth . . . "*Consentio.*"

As Uisdean MacUalraig was rising the young-looking vivacious canon called out – "What saith the prophet Ezekiel? *As I live, saith the Lord, I desire not the death of the wicked, but that the wicked turn from his way and live. Turn ye, turn ye from your evil ways.*"

The square red-faced canon on the Bishop's extreme right immediately rumbled, looking out from under his brows – "And doth not St Peter say in his Epistle: *The Lord delayeth not his promise, as some imagine, but dealeth patiently for your sake, not willant that ony suld. perish, but that all suld return to penance."*

The Bishop nodded affirmatively then glanced over at the theologian, inviting him to continue.

Uisdean MacUalraig resumed: "An it please you, my lord, the passage cited proves nothing that is nocht a part of Christian doctrine. The Catholic Kirk has aye held that the saints are predestined. But equally it has aye condemnit the added doctrine of reprobation from eternity, whilk is heretical. As lang syne as the year of Our Lord, five-hunder and twenty-nine, at the Second Council of Orange, it was declarit: *We not only refuse to believe that some men are by divine power predestined to evil, but an there be ony that hauld sic a wicked thing, we condemn them with utter detestation."*

"Amen," said the Bishop, "and rightly sae."

"This, my lord," the theologian continued, "is the doctrine of the heretic Calvin, and it is easily refuted baith from Revelation and from Tradition. As to Revelation, it runs counter to aa those mony texts of Scripture which assert the universality of God's saving will, the bestowal of sufficient grace upon all sinners, and the divine attribute of holiness. As to Tradition, the Fathers are of ane voice in upholding the orthodox teaching of the Kirk. The only ane wham the adherents of Predestinarianism hae daured to claim is St Augustine. Yet the Doctor of Grace expressly teaches: *God is guid, God is just. He can deliver some without merits because He is guid; but he cannot damn ony without demerits, because He is just.* St Prosper re-echoes this teaching when he says of the reprobates: *Of their ain will gaed they out: of their ain will they fell; and because their will was foreknown, they were not predestined. They would, however, be predestined if they were to return and persevere in holiness; hence God's predestination is for mony the cause of perseverance, for nane the cause of falling away.* St Fulgentius also expresses himself in like words . . . "

"H'm, h'm!" . . . The acid precise canon sitting on the Bishop's right hand broke in – "An it please you, my lord, the baxter himsel stands in ane analogy! Your lordship sincerely wills his liberation, but he will have nane of it, and sae, if he persist, it micht be said he is nocht predestined to be set at liberty. If, however, he acknowledge his error and cease from the propagation of harmful doctrine, he would be liberated, and in that case he would be predestined to liberation."

The Bishop inclined his head sideways but without taking his eyes from the heretics . . . "Preceesly, Canon!" Raising his hand he waved down what further Uisdean MacUalraig was about to say and went on . . .

"Weil, Cock, your weary doctrine stands condemnit by the Scriptures, and by the Fathers and the Tradition of the Kirk. And lest there suld yet be doubt upon thee, I will now declare to thee with authority, by virtue of mine office as ane bishop and pastor, what is the mind of the Kirk in this matter. It is nocht given to ony man to ken on earth what souls have gane or will gang to perdition, but this we hauld siccarly, by the surety we possess of God's honour and justice, that ilk ane lost is lost by his ain choice; that the mercy of God is toward all His creatures, and nane inherits the lot of the damned save him that casts awa God's mercy, kennin fu weel what it is he casts awa, and choosing to be cut off from the light of God rather than forswear his sinful will. Wha says contrariwise says heresy, and would imperil the souls of Christians with despair, whereas hope is necessary for salvation. Now, Cock, will ye receive the truth, or will ye persist in error?"

The baker's brow was overcast with a hue of vexation,

his voice was angry – "Nae doubt but ye are heich, nae doubt but ye are lifted up, that sit in pride and purple! But we have seen as heich and heicher evened with the lowermaist, when the arm of the Lord was suddenly streekit forth: and ye are but ane Herod for aa that, and the worms are ready that will devour ye!" He jumped up, thrusting out his chest, and shouted, with blazing eyes – "I will receive naething from thee, thou son of Belial, save submission to the Elect and their doctrine, whilk is God's doctrine! Yea, of a surety, do unto me what ye will that am led as a lamb to the slaughter, and like unto a sheep that is dumb afore her shearers, for I will not withhauld the testimony of my blude that it may rise up against you and your Chapter of idolaters!" He seemed to become infuriated, shrieking – "And abune aa I will hear nae mair of your Fathers, nay, nor your mothers, nor yet your sons and dochters! I will not admit even the angels of God that they suld judge my doctrine! But I will hae the Scriptures, and I will hae the Word of God, and *that* I will hae, and by that alane will I be judged!"

The friar cried again . . . "*Consentio!*"

The baker having sat down, noticing that some froth had fallen on his beard, swept it away with a casual downward motion of his open hand.

2

THE canon with the silver hair, on the Bishop's left, still smiling his old-man's smile, made a tut-tutting sound with his tongue, and with eyes closed, shook his head slowly from side to side. The young looking, ruddy canon beside him gave a shrug and a grimace, and looked at his neighbour on the left, who avoided his glance, stroking his forehead with his fingertips. The acid-precise canon on the Bishop's right was looking on the floor, drawing his fingers with a pulling motion down the ridge of his thin nose: while the square red-faced canon beside him, who had the look of a certain kind of very straightforward, unsubtle man, was simply staring out under his overhanging eyebrows. The Bishop was compressing his lips, and seemed in some doubt, or swither of impulse or intention, with regard to the heretics, studying meanwhile the causes of his offence. Uisdean MacUalraig was also studying them, with his mild, open glance: already that curious air, or remoteness, or insensibility of their predicament, had returned upon them. The baker appeared to be travelling emptily around over the stained stonework of floor and fretted walls.

The Bishop seized his course, having to get on with it, picked up the paper from where it had been lying on his knees, and clearing his throat twice loudly, so that the sound re-echoed, read out in his former judicial tone, but this time frowning –

"Secondly, Alexander Cock, these words: *Neither contrition, nor penance, nor ony other virtue, but faith alane is the medium or instrument by the whilk we are justifeed, and apprehend the grace of God, the merits of Christ and the remission of sins; guid works in particular are nocht but filthy clouts, righteousnesses of Pharisees and derogatory to the merits of Christ.*"

"Did ye say that, Cock?"

"I baith said it and will say it again."

The friar . . . "*Et ego consentio!*"

The Bishop moved his eyes round to Uisdean MacUalraig. "He'll no tak the Scriptures *and* the Fathers: e'en gie him the Scriptures *without* the Fathers."

Uisdean MacUalraig rose . . . "My lord . . . The teaching of the Scriptures in regard to the pairts played by faith and guid works in the process of justification may be summarised thus: first, a man may believe ilk article of our religion and yet be lost for want of guid works or because he hath not the love of God. Consequently, faith alane does not justifee nor insure eternal salvation. Our Divine Saviour Himself declared: *Not everyone that saith to me, Lord, Lord, sall enter into the kingdom of heaven, but he that doeth the will of my Father who is in heaven, he sall enter into the kingdom of heaven.* St James saith: *Do ye not see that by works a man is justifeed, and not by faith alane?* And St Paul: *If I suld have all faith, so that I could remove mountains, and have not charity, I am nothing . . .* Second, forbye faith, justification requires certain other preparatory or dispositive acts. There is, for example, the fear of divine justice; as it saith in Ecclesiasticus: *He that is without fear can nocht be justifeed.* Also, hope in God's mercy; as in Romans: *For we are saved by hope.* Again, charity; as in Luke: *Mony sins are forgiven her because she hath luvit much.* Furthermore, contrition or penitence; as in Luke again: *Unless ye sall do penance, ye sall all likewise perish.* Finally, guid works in general; as in St James: *So faith also, if it have not works, is dead in itself.*" He turned and faced the heretics, and said in a reasonable tone – "Nane that ponders these and other sic texts can maintain, as do Calvin and others, that the guid works mentioned merely accompany justification, for they are unmistakably describit as causes whilk dispose and prepare the sinner for it." He faced back to the Bishop – "Third, it is nocht faith alane that justifees, but faith informit and actuated by charity. As it saith in Galatians: *For in Christ Jesus neither circumcision availeth onything, nor uncircumcision; but faith that worketh by charity.* The Greek text, my lord, shows that the word *operatur* in the Vulgate maun be tane passively, so that a mair correct version of the same wad be 'but faith effected or formit by charity'. But the meaning is in substance the same, that is, a deid faith, withouten charity, availeth nothing. As St James saith: *For even as the body wanting the spirit is deid, so also faith without works is deid.* And soothly, my Lord, the Epistle of St James might be taen throughout as ane refutation in general of the doctrine of justification by faith without works."

The baker gave a superior shrug and ejaculated – "James is ane Epistle of Strae!"

"Now he'll no hae the Apostles!" remarked the young-looking ruddy canon aside.

The baker heard: he sprang up – "I will hae ane Apostle! And I will hae Paul when he says in the Romans: *For we account a man to be justifeed by faith alane – without the works of the Law!*"

The Bishop sat forward – "What's that? 'Faith alane'? Do I gang to schule to the heretics?"

The young-looking ruddy canon was laughing silently. Uisdean MacUalraig himself smiled. He said: "The word 'alane' does not occur in the texts, my lord. It was inserted by the heretic Luther, wha sought thereby to establish his doctrine by deceiving the ignorant, and is ane of the alterations or glosses in those heretical Scriptures whase reading in consequent is forbidden the laity. The context shows that it is a falsification. The Apostle contrasts justifying faith, not with those acts preparatory of salvation which spring from it, but with the barren 'works of the law', that is, of the Auld Testament, which, as sic, possessed nae mair power to justifee than the guid works of the heathen. This was pointed out lang syne by St Augustine, whom I cite not as a Father, but because he states the question mair clearly than it is my puir talent to do. 'Unintelligent persons,' quoth St Augustine, 'with regard to the Apostle's statement: *We conclude that a man is justifeed by faith*

without the works of the Law, have thocht him to mean
that faith is sufficient for a man, even if he leads a bad
life and has no guid deeds to allege. It is impossible that
sic a character suld be deemed 'a vessel of election' by
the Apostle, wha after declaring that 'in Christ neither
circumcision availeth onything nor uncircumcision,' adds
the important remark 'but faith that worketh by charity.' It
is sic faith that separates the faithful children of God from
unclean devils – for even these 'believe and tremble', as the
Apostle James saith, but they do no guid works. Therefore
they possess not the faith by the whilk the just man lives
– the faith which operates through luve in sic wise that
God recompenses it accordant til its works with eternal
life'. Thus St Augustine."

He was proceeding, but the Bishop, who had begun
to look fatigued, held up his hand.

"See where ye stand now, Cock," he said. "Ye hae
putten forrit twa propositions – the first, that the Scriptures
are the sole authority for Christians; the second, that
justification is by faith alane, without charity and guid
works. And the tane of your propositions has killed the
tither. Whilk of the twa will ye now renounce, therefore;
for since justification by faith alane is condemnit by the
Scriptures, ye maun either now gie up the Scriptures as
your authority or else forswear your doctrine of salvation
by faith alane."

The thin voice of the canon with the silver hair broke
in. " 'Tis dangerous, 'tis very dangerous!"

All looked at him.

He was looking straight before him dreamily, and
appeared to be reflecting aloud . . . "Wha then will
avoid sin or work guid til his neighbour? They say the
heretics say: *Pecca fortiter et crede firmius*!" He relapsed
into silence, shaking his head.

The square red-faced canon rumbled in his bass – "But, my lord, but this is a new thing, and nocht faith! Faith – the faith necessary for salvation – has aye been understandit as ane act of the intellect, assenting to the truths revealed by God. The heretics would even it with *fiducia*, whilk is not *faith* but *trust* or *confidence* – ane act of the will therefore, not of the intellect!"

"Aye, that is it!" exclaimed Uisdean MacUalraig involuntarily, recognising what he had himself been about to say. The Bishop glanced at him, then back at the heretics.

"Weil, Cock! " he said. "I await your answer!"

"I will answer ye!" said the baker getting up, flushed as it seemed for the moment even more with vexation than with anger. "And I will ask you, where gat *ye* the spirit of interpretation that ye suld declare unto *me* the interpretation of Haly Writ?"

The young-looking vivacious canon snorted and sat forward – "Where gat *ye* that spirit, that ye suld declare it unto *us*?"

The baker had barely reached his seat: he straightened again – "Wha but the sancts of God, suld hae the power to interpret the Word of God!"

"Are ye then sancts already?".

The baker set his shoulders and with head held back glanced down along his nose – "Thou hast said it!"

The square canon rumbled, "Show us your surety!"

The baker lifted up his eyes on him. "*The Spirit itself beareth witness with our spirit that we are the children of God,*" he quoted. "And by that Spirit do we declare and make known the Truth unto you that are hauden in darkness, if sae be your darkness may be lichted up by the licht that is in huz!"

The Bishop snorted in turn. "Man, Cock! ye pass

aa! *We* interpret Scripture by nane inward and private,
and therefore uncertain illumination; but openly, by the
light of Reason, and conform to the harmony of doctrine
in its divers parts, and under the authority of the Kirk.
(And, mark you, Cock, the Kirk has the richt to interpret
Scripture, for it is the Kirk that guarantees the authority
of Scripture, which indeed was first written in proof and
witness of the doctrines of the Kirk.) But ye, Cock, in
despite of Reason, wad mak the Scriptures witness til
their ain authority. – Nothing, nor no man, Cock, can
witness til his ain authority; but all authority, save only
God, is witnessed til from without and from above – (it
is not what *I* say – as if *I* were somebody – but what I say
that is accordant to Reason, or what I say by virtue of the
authority gien me by another, whase authority, in turn, is
establishit.) But ye, Cock, when bidden show your title
to interpret Scripture, point – not to that without, that
might guarantee it – but to your ain breist – as if there was
ocht in there but wind and your mislearit heart! My word
upon it, Cock, ye weary me! Argue your case nor prove
yoursel ye cannot; ye but assert and play the oracle. And
your emptiness of sound reason ye are fain to cloak with
a windy sough of words!"

The baker had risen. He was crimson. Pushing backwards the fists he held clenched by his sides and bending
himself forward, he shouted, shaking his beard at the
clerics – "Stuffed cassocks! Whited walls! Speak ye to me
of Reason! What, i' faith, is Reason?" – with hands and
eyes seeking an answer from the surrounding air – "Reason
is a whure! Reason is the Devil's greatest whure!" – setting
his arms akimbo and advancing his side-face – "Does the
Reason gie licht? Aye, verily, like the licht dung would gie
forth were it putten in a lanthorn!"

He stopped abruptly, opening his eyes wide. His

mouth fell open. A smile had appeared on every face! The young ruddy-faced canon was laughing outright and without disguise, throwing back his head. The silver-haired canon wore a bland smile on his blind-looking upturned face, while the robust recently fiery-haired canon at the end of the row put up his hand along his brow to screen his features while his shoulders trembled. The acid-precise canon had again taken his thin nose in his finger-tips, and was looking at the ground aside, his cheeks filling spasmodically behind his close-pressed lips. Even the Bishop allowed himself a small smile that turned down the corners of his mouth.

The heavy, somewhat puzzled look had lifted for the first time from the square canon's red face at the end of the row nearest the door. His nostrils twitched and his eyes twinkled under their over-hanging brows as he rumbled –

"How cam ye to that about the Reason, Cock? By the use of reason, or without? If by reason your judgment maun be fause, since accordant to you ain sel, ye have won til't by the use of ane incapable instrument – the Reason. Your statement – do ye no see? – contradicts itsel, since ere it could be true the Reason would need to gie ye licht eneugh at least to show ye it gies nane . . . Or do ye admit that without reason ye hae condemned the Reason?"

The ruddy young-looking canon laughed – "Nae reasonable road from Reason, Cock. 'Tis what ye ca' a *'sequitoorie'*."

The baker, with an eagle eye glancing from one to the other, tightly pursing his lips, was suddenly shaken like a wisp.

"Lauch! Lauch, sons of Belial," he shrieked, while the beard trembled on his quaking jaw – "Lauch, children of perdition! Whuremongers! Idolaters! Unclean! Lauch, ye

limbs of Satan! worshippers of the Abomination! Bloody
persecutors! Aye, lauch – but the day cometh, and is now
come, when He that sitteth in the heavens sall lauch! Yea,
verily, the judgment is e'en now without the door! Ye will
be bound thegether like faggots to be cast intil the furnace
of the wrath of God" – his feverish, sunken eyes fixing
upon the Bishop – "Aye, and you also, my lord Bishop,
even you, together with your lordship's bastards and their
dam the painted Jezebel that lay in your lordship's bed!"

3

THE Bishop's cheeks trembled, turning purple. "*A
veechk!* . . ." he spat forth, then cut the words off at
the lips and sat lowering. Something passing across his
face seemed to wipe the features to a hardness as of
rock. His eyes had become small and hard above their
pouches.

"Cock," he said at last impressively in a voice that
trembled, "I give you my word that when first I heard
your doctrines it gaed across my mind that you maun
be in jest, though the jest, i' faith, was ill chosen. I ken
now it was nae jesting with you – and pity it is, and pity
for all your crew, for could ye jest ye wad ne'er wander
sae far from all reason and guid sense. Natheless although
ye cannot jest I trow ye be ower light-minded. Here ye
stand chargit with a crime that by the law of this realm
is to be punishit with death. So ye might truly be said
here to stand in the ante-chamber of the Judgment. An
ye prove-na mair tractable ye may stand afore your Maker
– aye, ere twa suns have set – to thole His dread assize
and answer for the haill sins committed in your life. Yet
sae light-minded are ye, ye bear yoursel as if ye were but
flyting in the mercat-place, and your meat waited ye on the
buird at your ain fireside. First ye put forrit doctrines baith

absurd and damnable; syne when it is faithfully shown ye
they are no maintainable, instead of retracting them as
would a guid-willant reasonable man, ye change about to
hurling accusations on the ground of morals – (*He that is
without sin, let him first cast the stane!*) Twa things suld
be evident, even til an unlearit man, for sic ye truly say
ye are: the first, that the truth and salutary nature of
sound doctrine are nocht impugnit by the moral state of
its defenders and representatives; the second, that when
ye come to answer for your ain sins it will nocht avail
ye to cite the douncomings of others, though they were
those of a bishop. Standing as ye are on the doorstane of
the Judgment it behoves ye weel to accuse yoursel afore
your ain conscience, if sae be it will stead ye better when
ye face your reckoning. Yet of this ye show nae sense, as
if ye had nocht to answer for; or – what seems mair likely –
as if your inward state was the maist real and present thing
with ye, and dulled perception of the position in the whilk
ye stand.

"Cock, I look at ye and I wonder. What is it that
ails ye? Did ye in truth seek pure doctrine, and that out
of a pure heart and unfeignit mind, ye would embrace
it gladly. But you when ye are gien pure doctrine will
no receive it – nay, but haud the mair to that whilk is
fause. So then I perceive it is not pure doctrine that ye
crave, and for the sake of pure doctrine – ye hae deceived
us there, and wad deceive others, making a profession –
but what ye seek is something other, something that ye
hope to gain *by means of fause doctrine*. If sae, we but
waste wind upon ye, for your heresy lies not within the
mind but abides in some distemper of your will, in your
desires and your affections.

"Cock, I hae dealt fairly by ye. I will do fairer yet. I
will say in charity that ye may be a pure soul, and that ye

may have been offended by the conduct of some. So far as I am accused in person ye do me less than justice. It is true that when a youth, and afore ever I was a priest, I was handfasted, and of that union had issue like another. If it was a sin in me, though sanctioned by the custom of the realm, I was guilty of it; and I sall answer for it afore Him Wha will yet judge me and all men. But of other sin of like carnal nature afore God I declare me innocent. But there are others – aye, shame that I suld say it, even in this diocese! – whase conversation has been neither lawful nor circumspect, unworthy pastors of God's flock, whase courses have offendit 'little anes' of tender conscience – sic like, it might be, as yoursel . . .

"Cock, I will mak a bargain with ye. Your doctrines are damnable, for they impugn the chiefest tenet of our holy religion, the luve of God and His saving will towards all our sinful human kind. And they will be interpret by mony in the sense that guid works are of nane account, and so against law and conscience they will fall in sins for which, repenting not, they may be damned. Ye will see that ye canna be looten lowse to sow despair of God's mercy among puir souls that we haud it in commission to protect against pernicious error; and to gie cause to some whereby they will damn their sowls. For to spread heresy, Cock, besides a crime afore the law, is the greatest of aa the sins against our neighbour, since it consists in perilling his chances of eternal blessedness. Sae I will strike ane compact with ye . . . They say ye mak guid breid . . . Gie me your solemn word to keep your notions to yoursel in your ain bakehoose till ye come to see mair reason. And for my part – though some clergy be bad, yet there be mony guid – gie me your word to quell your tongue, and I will gie ye my word, that as it hath been my labour heretofore, sae and even mair sall it be my labour henceforward, that the guid will be suffered and the evil sall be reformed, an I brook life!"

The baker got up. He started calmly . . . "I will mak nane bond with the mammon of iniquity" – but immediately blazed up, holding his face sideways and throwing forward a threatening and accusing forefinger – "nay, nor with thee, thou braying ass! And the mair as, though ye ken it not, it rests not in your hands to fill ane compact. Life does not remain to ye to reform ocht. For the judgment against idolaters has gane forth, the writing is on the wall against ye! Woe to thee, thou bloody man, when the suffering sancts of God put their hands to the work, and the judgment of the Righteous sall be executed upon thy body!"

The Bishop, having leant back in his seat, moved his hand and said wearily: "If I be even as you say, ane ass, and if ye be a prophet as ye appear to think, let me remind you there was a time already when *a dumb ass, speaking with man's voice, rebuked the madness of a prophet.*" He roused himself and sat forward – "And if they be threats against me that ye have uttered, I am nothing daunted, though some among ye be men of blude that work by stealth. I did not put on this purple for a decoration to my person, I have wrocht a lang day in the vineyard – let my deeds testifee! – and if impious men, traitors to God and their country, would tak awa my life, I will round it out like ane true Scot and ane leal son of Holy Kirk – and I will have this purple for my shroud!"

He sat back . . . "However, Cock, that day is na yet, and I am nocht here to be judged by you, but ye are here to be judged by me."

He took up from his knee the bill of indictments as if to read the next in order of the heretical propositions. But groaned . . .

"Och! there's a great mony things here yet!" – and lowered it, saying, "What boots it? Enow is enow!"

Holding the paper straight out towards the heretics and assuming a judicial voice, he said, "Alexander Cock! Ye have uttered heresy in the hearing of all present, and I solemnly charge thee now, wilt thou recant these propositions, keeping weil in mind, if no, that under the law of this realm the crime is punishable with death." He added, "An ye will crave time . . ."

The baker stood up.

"I want nane," he said without excitement, and indeed a kind of pride and dignity. "Neither for thee nor for all the devils in Hell, will I recant ane word of what *ye* call heresy, but what I call Christ's Evangel, the message of saving grace poured out upon us wha are God's Elect, chosen in Him afore the beginning of the world!"

"It sufficeth!"

The Bishop opened his hand. The Paper of the indictment, after two fluttering swoops this way and that, skimmed sailingly away above the floor and fell lightly to rest not far in front of the heretics' feet.

The Bishop rose up, very solemnly. "Alexander Cock! I pronounce you guilty of heresy, I can do no other . . . "

A shout from the baker went up . . . "The water, my lord! Ye forget the water!"

The Bishop stopped. Everyone looked with surprise at the baker, who sat, still wearing his air of pride and dignity, his head held high.

"Aye!" said he, folding his arms and with head slightly aside glancing at the wall – "Bid them bring in the water!" – with an ironical twist of his mouth – "This is the place! . . . 'Tis in the play!"

All around the expressions relaxed in understanding,

with glances of reproof or scorn. The Bishop said testily
– "I am nae mair Pilate than ye are Christ; ye speak
blasphemously in imputing it to yoursel . . . " Reassuming
his judicial tone, he said . . . "I pronounce you, Alexander
Cock, guilty of heresy, and I now relax you to the secular,
to be taen back from whence ye cam and there to underlie
the law!"

The baker, seated in his place, raised a harsh exultant
shout. "Yea, of a surety, truly is it written: *For thy sake
we are putten to death aa the day lang. We are accounted
as sheep for the slaughter.*"

The Bishop raised his hand palm outward before his
face, turning his head away – "Cock, ye deave me!"

But then he turned back, and stood, with a penetrating and discerning look fixed on the baker . . .

"Ye hae rejected the Kirk, and the Fathers, and the
faculty of Reason, and the Scriptures unless ye be looten
wrest them as it suits ye – rejected, in guid sooth, aathing
except Cock!"

He paused, narrowing his eyes. His hands clenched
themselves. With head and shoulders thrust forward in the
direction of the baker – "Cock!" he said, with an accent of
intensity, "I ken ye now! . . . Ye are aa cocks thegether
– *and ye wad mak a midden o Scotland so that ye might
craw on the tap o't!*"

He turned to go. The canons had also risen; their
unequal height was seen. The acid-precise canon in the
Bishop's path said: "H'm, h'm, my lord, what of the friar
Coltart? Will ye examine him, or as he has subscribit the
heresies of the other sall he also be adjudged guilty?"

The Bishop stopped, and turning again bulkily, fixed
a long, heavy look on the friar, expression draining from
his eyes. And pronounced . . . "*Consentio!*"

The friar had throughout given the impression of

trying to thrust himself forward into the proceedings, by
way of his unasked-for comments and a certain something
forced and exaggerated in his postures and facial expressions of indifference or disdain. Now he leapt up as if
stung. They heard him catch his breath. His inch-long
beard bristled, his blue eyes paling in his flaming face.
Casting a venomous, reproachful, hurt, offended look at
the Bishop, he scraped his foot across the floor.

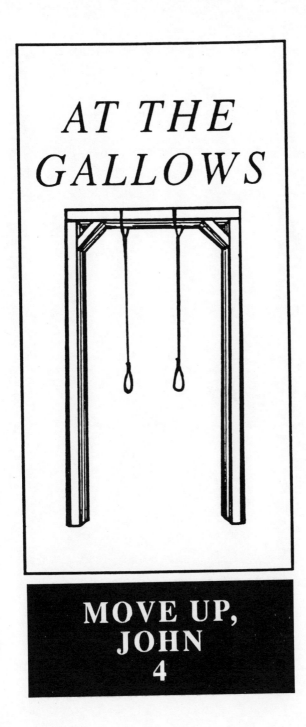

AT THE GALLOWS

MOVE UP, JOHN
4

PART FOUR

T HE HANDFUL OF WOMEN washing clothes by
the river stopped and straightened themselves to
look in startled surprise at the little priest, John
Tod, with his flaming hair, walking so fast that he was
nearly running. One glimpse only they caught of his pale
features, working with emotion, and then immediately
found themselves looking at his slight form diminishing
rapidly each time his back flashed into view among the
bushes. Then he had gone from sight: there was only the
smooth, dark river, the grassy bank by their side with
its green bushes, and, above, the tall grey masonry of
silent buildings that was the town. And already it seemed
doubtful if he had ever appeared suddenly as if from
nowhere and gone rushing past at all . . .

He was unable to moderate his headlong pace and
scarcely knew where he was. Never had there been such
a tempest in him. He could not manage it. It was sweeping
him away. If he had only just witnessed the first dawn of
all breaking upon the world – if he had just received his
sight – everything could not have appeared more strangely
new and as if never seen before. Where, then, had he
been all his life till now? In some kind of sleep, some

aboriginal oblivion. He was sick with perturbation. An exultation the source of which he feared to recognise was lifting him up, threatening to sweep him away from all solidness of custom, so that he clung to his terror as to a line to safety. He was afraid to know what had come upon him, even while simultaneously deep down within he cloudily recognised it, like something that had always been in him. He felt himself at the same time frantic for flight and delirious to be possessed – as he knew he *could* be utterly, irrevocably possessed. Every successive instant he seemed to be making in himself acts of flight that were at once desperate and half-hearted, yet knowing himself somehow, not without fearful exultation, too much possessed already. What he had been heretofore he felt to be already shattered in him beyond recall by what had with such utter unexpectedness, so totally without warning, leapt upon him: knowing himself, with regret and hesitations and a still wilder hope, all given over in the end of this possession to appointed signal change, from which he shrank even while he seemed to fly to meet it.

As if duplicating the dialectic of his wild emotions in a different notation, of material things-seen, the same succession of tumbling images went continuously through his brain . . .

Again the gabled houses stood around the market-place. Their grey fronts hard in the cold light from an even sky – grey, midday light, equally diffused everywhere, yet bright too, lacking but a very little brightness to throw shadows. There was a little dry wind (he could feel it again): in sunken places among the cobbles pools were three-quarters dried, with wide, damp margins: the damp margins, and the surface of the pools themselves, covered over with a thick sprinkling of dust. At the house windows were heads looking down at people in the square, or gaping at the gallows. Every minute more appeared at windows and more moved into the square from all directions till the space was loosely filled. Clusters gathered on the fore-stairs: some people had brought out stools and benches and were standing on them against the house walls.

Now again the procession came into view, with crowds of people on either side by the walls keeping pace, some running on ahead. The cart was rocking and jolting, drawn forward over the stones with a trundling motion. The baker was standing in it, and with lifted head never ceased, in spite of the jostling, to apostrophise the fronts of the houses above the heads of the hurrying people. On the opposite side the friar was still in his soiled habit and broad leather belt. He was leaning his elbow on the top-bar of the cart, one foot crossed over the other and with one hand placed with the broad fingers spread above his stout buttock, looking at the people jostling alongside with a superior, amused smile in his half-grown beard. On the shaft the sardonic figure of the hangman was sitting. While he idly swung his leg, a straw jumped up and down at the corner of his mouth. Every now and then he flicked his whip negligently at the horse's thick flanks, while his eyes with a sardonic twinkle returned to the people hurrying and pushing along.

All this appeared with a preternatural clearness to John Tod's perceptions, which became painfully sharpened as he felt and saw the approach of the fearful unknown – heresy! – though doomed here to a violent end. He could not take it in that he was here seeing face to face, though cushioned by the great company of watchers, that dreaded element of revolt against the order of God and man, the present cause of all upheaval and disquiet, that insane courage to assert the wrong even to the verges of the Pit, threatening the whole structure civil and spiritual in which he was a secure if inwardly unquiet point. This instant anticipation imparted to him so tingling a sense of being present, so sharpened his perception and consciousness of time and place, that the gabled houses, clear in the moving air, stood solid as if with expectation; the faces round him suddenly appeared sculpturesque, as if incarnating some heretofore unguessed reality within their commonplaceness. The quips and jests being tossed around all at once carried to his ears oracular echoes. Even the powdering over the half-dried pools might have been compounded with dust of eternity. But partaking more than anything of the two intermingled worlds – factual-temporal and significant-eternal – were the ropes dangling high not far from each other, ending in twin nooses swaying a little in the occasional gusts of the dry wind, and the dry faggots prepared below.

The market-place had become filled to capacity. There was pushing towards the front. The two men in the dress of countrymen jostled him in their eagerness to have a good view of what was forward, looking all round them, talking together in Scottish. Then they found themselves next to a townsman of their acquaintance in tradesman's dress, and the conversation became English, and in that new, sharpened sense of his, even the names by which they called each other seemed suddenly redolent of their essence – as if they might have been the names by which they were known to God.

The countryman next John Tod stretched his red and weatherbeaten neck past his companion towards the townsman.

"Wha's for the tow the-day, Henrick?"

And the second countryman, standing dumpily between them, opined . . . "A pickle thieves, nae doubt!"

"Waur nor that," came the townsman's voice with

overtones of patronage and waggery – the townsman to the rustic. "It's twa that brocht the plague."

"The plague . . . ! shairly no the plague!" exclaimed the countrymen simultaneously.

"E'en sae! The plague, and waur nor the plague . . . It's heresy, that's what it is!"

"Heresy! *Here*?" – the countrymen looked at each other and fell silent, furtively crossing themselves.

"Wha is 't?" said the one next John Tod, awed, stretching his weather-beaten neck again.

"Wha is't?" The townsman's laugh sounded out. "Tak a glisk of yon speakin chiel! I'se warrant ye ken him!"

The procession was in the square. A silence had fallen in which the creaking of axles and rasping of wheels against cobble-stones could be heard – and above it all a voice, high-pitched in continuous exulting . . .

"Swounds!" exclaimed the countryman. "It's the baxter!"

"E'en sae," said the townsman. "The baxter, wha but he!"

"But it canna be! A heretic? I ken him weil!"

"No that weil, Rob, syn ye ken-na him for a heretic!"

"What cry ye him?" said the countryman in the middle.

"Cock," came the townsman's voice from farthest off. "Sanders Cock, and a prophet amang them, or they lee that tell it."

"And I never kent it!" The countryman beside John Tod was gasping in incredulity . . . "Certes, he was aye a lang-gabbit chiel, and an unco lowe in his ee. But a heretic! And eke a prophet!"

He lent an ear a moment to the baker, and made a noise indicating contempt. Without looking to see who his neighbour was on that side he made a wide bucolic sweep of his elbow and smote John Tod in the chest, saying gutturally, through barely opened lips . . . "This Cock will get his caim crappit!"

Though it had made him stagger he had scarcely felt that elbow. That was the instant when his attention had been utterly arrested. The baker had come into plain view . . . and his face showed him beatified. After the first silence cries had broken out in the crowd; from all directions jeers were hurled at the occupants of the cart, till there was a roar of execration. But unabated the baker's testifying rose over all. When his burning eyes lit on the sea of faces, the gallery of heads looking from every window, he was renewed in vehemence, visibly exalted. Their hostility was matter of indifference. Jolting forward he was struck above the eye with an egg, but paid no attention except to wipe away the fluid that ran down his face and obscured his sight . . . And as he spoke all the high things of the world came tumbling down, and every topmost stone was laid lower than the lowermost, the mighty of the land left their places, the exalted were abased, mitred heads rolled in the dust, and the mouths were stopped of those that sat above and taught the people. And taking scope through that universal downfall the doctrine of the pure Word filled the land, and the Elect, its oracles, mounted to the places left vacant by the fallen mighty . . . And in a moment it became felt that there was another element besides offence and absurdity in the situation, and after its first outburst the mirth and jeering moderated itself before the spectacle of a greater ecstasy. That of a slight figure in the hangman's cart, the fluid contents of an egg on his sunken cheeks and, with fragments of shell in his thin beard, while a flush glorified his brow, and over his head, and on his behalf, there was not the gallows, but a blowing of trumpets, a breaking of seals, and the pouring forth of the vials of the wrath of God upon his Persecutors. Some in the unprecedented spate were open-mouthed like fish. But there were exclamations of pity mingled with the declining hootings in the crowd. This he witnessed – Cock exalted, and all in sight, or hearing of his voice, subdued. The buildings around were suddenly shaken in the beatings of his heart. His soul had come to his eyes and looked out upon the market-place – *and the market-place looked into his soul.* Everything thereafter that took place out there in the market-place was even more a happening in his soul.

All at once it was another than Cock that was climbing the ladder to the scaffold . . . more striking-looking than Cock, with flaming hair, and of a greater unction. Without surprise he saw it was himself. He it was who was standing now aloft on a high place, speaking and gesturing with more vehemence, greater oracular power, his words a more torrential downpour, more than Cock the centre and wonder of every living eye, the source of greater and more silent awe and more unquestionably the greater man in sight . . .

But icy tremors gripped him. His eye fell on the noose. And the faggots waiting. He was aware of that old familiar torment of vexed tears. When he looked again he saw that he had vanished from the scene, as smoothly and silently as he had appeared. Cock and the other stood high on the scaffold, in a hush of expectation. The moment was approaching that would silence them forever, and their new way. He saw the friar, planted sideways, staring fixedly, as if all the heads below did not exist, at the sheet that with a bursting effect of whiteness flowed out at that minute like a signal flag from the topmost window of the house facing him, the house of the merchant, Inglis, largest in the square. Cock, heedless of that or anything, was declaiming still with unabated unction . . . a prophecy of bloody swords upon his persecutors. Not in the future time but *now*, upon the instant. His hand rose high: he brought his eyes down upon the people: in the hush his words were heard and their echo in the farthest corners of the square . . .

"Hearken e'en now and hear the feet of them that hasten to avenge God's persecuted Holy Ones!"

In the dismayed silence were veritably heard approaching hoof-falls – his heart began to throb again; himself to hanker – his form to appear and re-appear with tentative standing – on the scaffold. Now there was shouting beyond the houses, shouting with a slightly strange, deliberate-sounding echo – like a chorus of avengers in a play. Screams and frantic shouting from the merchant's windows, and from here and there throughout the crowd, of the dreaded name – 'Pitfourie!' – set off the panic surging away and scattering. Even as there were armed men on horses dancing in the square, and – veritably – Pitfourie, sitting his horse, with drawn sword, looking here and there. Not even turning his head when that mortal shriek of the hangman rent the air as some of them caught him on their spear points jumping from the scaffold . . .

He felt himself carried along, willy-nilly, in the flood. Looking backwards he saw last of all the two, descended from the scaffold, mounted on horses. The friar, a stout hairy leg protruding from under his habit, with a hand gingerly feeling at his throat. Cock still declaiming, turning round in the saddle towards the now empty square, his hand on high.

Or rather last of all as he was swept from the square his laggard eye fell on the twin gaping nooses. And therewith, his recollection carried back to the previous stage of the proceedings, when they were about to be placed round necks, in spite of himself chills ran through him again and checked an upward flowing tide.

But then once more there was the galloping – avenging shouts – and his head and breast were filled with horses and armed men. And they meant no longer chill and diminution but . . . at last . . . succour and protection, warmth – a bulwark and not a barrier. So well for this time: could it be always so . . . always the galloping of armed succour? Could he . . . ? What could he . . . ?

An acclamation that he recognised – it had shouted in him before, many times in the depths – had risen to be deafening, drowning the voice of everything in him besides. The rhythm of armies mounted up in him, tuned to the beating of his heart, which drove him onward to the settling point, both elate and shrinking. A sun-pricked height above a parting roof of cloud was dazzling him. But the leap . . . the leap!

The bushes kept bouncing towards him and he kept bouncing past them. He was on his feet. He scarcely knew it.

Oh . . . God . . . ! Where . . . ?

THE

DOUNCOME

MOVE UP,
JOHN
5

PART FIVE

I N THE CHURCH was a low, continuous hum. People were gathered throughout the nave, most numerously towards the altar end, or standing above the pillars or in the aisles. More people also continued to trickle in by the great doorway, who after crossing themselves and genuflecting towards the altar either remained kneeling, or seated themselves and looked around them, or approached one or other of the groups standing, with questioning looks and words. Nevertheless the variegated light from the deeply glowing windows lay over all, the masonry above and the heads below, with the effect of silence from a great distance.

By and by from up among the hollow places under the roof came a small booming sound of a door closing somewhere in the building. Uisdean MacUalraig who had been kneeling in the front raised his head and turned it from side to side, appearing to try to locate the sound; then got up and having bent his knee towards the altar turned about and came part way down the church and went in under the right-hand aisle to where he saw the sacristan standing in the shadow by the sacristy door.

"Weil?" He spoke urgently, almost sharply.

"Neither sight nor sound of him," replied the sacristan, plucking at his dark, square beard, "although he bade
ring the bells. But it was the Protestants that rade into the
toun; there's nae doubt about that."

Uisdean MacUalraig contracted his brows. What had
happened to John Tod? Had he perchance fallen into the
hands of the heretics? – he was very outspoken, impru-
dent, even violent when, breaking his usual brooding and
moody silence, he gave way to speech. He was worried
about him. But he had been worried about him for some
time. Some change had come over the man recently, some
change that he could not fathom. He had wondered at
times if perhaps the recent disorders and dangers were
unhinging his mind. He had always been moody and
self-absorbed, and now was more so than ever. But there
was at the same time a curious air like self-satisfaction,
almost a triumphant air, that he carried about with him.
He had lately surprised him once or twice looking at
him with a curious expression, as if he had some secret
knowledge that was giving him private delight, though
he at once shrouded his eyes on seeing that he was
observed. Perhaps his mind was really giving way a little
– he had always been somewhat strange, seemed to sit
uncomfortably or unhappily to circumstances, not to be
integrated with himself in his life . . . And then there
was the secrecy and mystery of his recent movements, his
obscure comings and goings, how he would be missing at
odd hours of the day or even the night, and returning give
no account of himself but immediately shut himself away.
What could be happening to him? He felt – had always
felt – somehow responsible for him. There was that priest,
Duncan Lindsay, stoned to death only the other day by
some rabble led on by the heretics. This disappearance
had an evil look.

"Ye are sure it was the Protestants that cam into the toun?"

"Althegether sure, Maister Uisdean, and Pitfourie the heid o them. And I sair misdoot mischief's intended. Pitfourie does naething for nae reason."

"If that is sae . . ." – Uisdean MacUalraig raised his head as if considering, or he might have been listening. His air became decided. "A surplice!" he said, with a quick snap of the fingers, turning towards the sacristy.

The hum died when the sacristan walked into the church. Uisdean MacUalraig walking behind him in white upon black. Eyes followed them as they went up on to the sanctuary and knelt bowed before the altar, the sacristan below and behind. When the priest straightened the other rose and placed a veil across his shoulders, and he stood up and approached the tabernacle. Silence became so intense in the church that there could be heard a small waxen popping of tapers burning somewhere before a shrine. A click from the tabernacle doors sounded fateful, and a sighing wave of sound swept along the floor as all in the church went to their knees. The sacristan in the renewed silence walked down from the altar, the priest, bowed over what he had held at his breast in his veil-shrouded hands, walking behind him all the way past the prostrate people and back into the sacristy.

The opened tabernacle remained gaping above the altar, and drew to itself the fascinated gaze of all, whom its emptiness more disturbed. But the priest had returned, black now in his cassock, walking purposefully, and crossing the church mounted into the pulpit. When he was seen standing there there was a rustling and moving, then silence.

"In the name of the Father, and of the Son, and of the Holy Ghost . . . "

Uisdean MacUalraig's voice was clear, though not loud: there was some drawing up towards the top of the church.

"Brethren,

"When Our Lord Jesus Christ at the first, before His Ascension into Heaven, laid upon the Apostles their mission in the world, the words that He used were these: *All power is given to me in heaven and in earth. Going therefore teach ye all nations, baptising them in the name of the Father, and of the Son, and of the Holy Ghost. Teaching them that they should observe all things whatsoever I have commanded you: and behold I am with you all days, even to the consummation of the world.*

"See here the warrant and commission of the Apostles, and of their successors the bishops and pastors of Christ's Kirk. Jesus Christ receivit from His Father *all power in heaven and in earth*: and per virtue of this power *He* sends *them – even as His Father sent Him*, as it saith in St John – *to teach* not ane but *all nations*, and to instruct them in *all truths*. And that He may assist them effectually in the execution of this His commission, He promises to be with them, not alane for the lifetime of the Apostles, not alane for three, or four, or ten generations, but *all days, even to the consummation of the world.*

"See here the Kirk's commission, laid upon it by God in the Person of His Son, and joinit thereto God's promise, whereby all men in all times may be assured that that whilk the Kirk teaches is the truth. And woe be unto us, brethren, woe be unto us if we do not God's bidding and proclaim not unto all men in all times these truths that were given unto us and were to be for the salvation of the world."

He placed his hands wide on the pulpit edge and leaned a little forward:

"But if it be the Kirk's mission to proclaim and teach the truth, it maun follow as a part of that same that it is Her duty to protect the truth which She proclaims, and preserve it from the errors to whilk the mind of man is in all ages and conditions prone. And so it is that in every age a part of the Kirk's activity, in the execution of Her commission, which She has from God, has aye had to be the combating of heresy.

"Now it is of heresy that I would speak. "

The silence intensified.

"Heresy, my dear sons and brethren, is not at the first sicht a simple thing to bring to judgment. For what is heresy, and what maks a heretic? A heretic, in the Greek from which the word comes, is 'ane that picks and chooses'; in matters of Faith it means ane that chooses out for himself doctrines that he will profess, rejecting others. And as the Roman poet has said, there are as mony opinions as there are men, so it needs nocht surprise us that there suld be nearhand as mony heresies as there be heretics. Now our desire is to come at some comprehension of what heresy is as a thing *in itsel*, and to that end it will nocht serve us to enumerate all the heresies and refute them ane by ane. For heresy is a Proteus – that was, a kind of monster – which changes its forms e'en as you grapple with it; or it is a monster of mony heids, each with a voice, so that even as you silence ane, ye are assailed by others. To the variety of heresy there is nane end, or the confusion of its voices.

"As therefore it would be thankless, as endless, to seek for the essence of heresy in the variety of its actual forms, let us rather see if there be not in all forms some constant or common element; if sae be that by consideration of what they have in common we may win til an understanding of the nature of the thing itsel. For

if there be that which heresy is *in itsel*, it will manifestly
be revealed in that respect in the whilk all heresies agree,
rather than in those mony in the whilk they differ.

"Now I am minded about twa things whereon it is
maist clearly to be seen that all heretics are of ane mind
thegether. Though they may differ on all things else – as
for instance on the Sacraments, some saying there are but
twa, others three, others five, and some nane – there are
twa things at least on the whilk all are agreed; and these
are, first, in that they deny that God our Lord is Really
Present in the Sacrament of the Altar, and second, in
refusing with an equal violence to honour Her wha is the
Mother of Christ, God the Son, come on earth in the form
of Man. Can that universal agreement of heretics on these
twa heids tell us ocht of the inward nature and essence of
heresy?

"Now as to the first, there has never been a time
when the Kirk has not held and taught that Christ is truly
and really present in this Blessed Sacrament – and I may
remind ye again of Christ's promise to preserve His Kirk
from error. But I pass that by, because, as we ken weil,
the heretics will not receive the authority of the Kirk.
Again, there is the experience of us, whose souls have
ere now been wounded unto life in the Communion of
this Sacrament, whereby our being has been filled with
His licht. But that also I pass by, for we ken also that no
heretic will abide the judgment or regard the experience
of another. But they claim to accept the Scripture, and
the judgment of the Scripture they maun therefore abide
whether they will or no.

"What then saith the Scripture? In the Holy Gospel
of St John we read these words: I am the living breid
which came doun from heaven. If ony man eat of this
breid, he sall live forever; *and the breid that I will give*

is my flesh, for the life of the world. The Jews therefore
strove among themsels, saying: How can this man gie us
his flesh to eat? Then Jesus said to them: Amen, amen,
I say to you: *Except ye eat the flesh of the Son of Man,
and drink his blude, ye sall not have life in you. He that
eateth my flesh, and drinketh my blude, hath everlasting
life; and I will raise him up in the last day. For my flesh is
meat indeed, and my blude is drink indeed. He that eateth
my flesh, and drinketh my blude, abideth in me, and I in
him. As the living father hath sent me, and I live by the
Father; sae also he that eateth me, the same also sall live
by me.*"

He paused, and with an extraordinary effect of
emphasis said quietly . . .

"My dear brethren, He that spake these words was
God. He baith said He was God and proved it by mony
miracles and chief of all by His rising from the tomb. If
these words be not true, God is a liar, and the haill body
of Christians from that day till this, have lived and died
in error, deceivit by their Creator. Nor will it avail to say,
as the heretics do, that He spake but in a figure. For if it
was sae then in a figure He deceivit His Apostles, and the
Kirk that he founded through them was founded by Him
in error, the while He gave them His promise to preserve
it in truth.

"Moreover it is recorded in the same place that: After
this mony of his disciples went back, and walked nae mair
with him. Do we then read that He recalled them, lest they
suld be deceived, not perceiving that He spake but in a figure? Nay, but lest they suld think He spake but in a figure
he had already confirmed His words with these: it is the
spirit that quickeneth; the flesh (meaning thereby man's
natural and carnal apprehension) profiteth nothing. *The
words that I have spoken to you, they are spirit and life.*

"And yet again, when He instituted the Eucharistic Sacrifice afore His Passion, it is recorded in the Gospels how He took breid, and blessed, and brake, and gave to His disciples, saying: Tak ye, and eat; *This is My Body*; and how, after, He took the chalice, and gave thanks, and gave to them, saying: Drink ye all of this, *for this is My Blude of the new testament,* which sall be shed for mony unto remission of sins – words usit in the Mass ilka day at the Consecration, in obedience to His injunction: *This do for a commemoration of me.* This, too, the heretics are fain to say, was but a figure; thus asking us to believe that in that solemn moment, afore He entered upon His Passion, Our Blessed Lord again deceivit His Apostles, with a figure. Thus too taking away from that scene in the upper room the only Meaning that would explain and justifee its solemnity.

"But I do not cite those passages, beloved brethren, in order to prove to you what ye already ken and believe, since ye are of those who, not being madmen, would rather believe God than man. I cite them in order to show beyond ony possibility of doubt that in denying that Christ is Really Present in this Breid of the altar the heretics fly full in the face of the very Scriptures on the whilk they claim to base themsels.

"Now we maun ask . . . Why? Why are the heretics, wha dispute amang themsels in baying against *this* doctrine, a doctrine not alane always and everywhere believit and taught by the Kirk, but also maist plainly affirmed by the Scriptures? For men wha believe in God, and that the Scriptures are from God, there is nae *reasonable* cause that they suld not believe in this doctrine. Why then do they all with ane accord, and that vehemently, refuse to believe it *against reason*?

"That they are offended at it is manifest. But *why* are

they offended? What is there in the doctrine, that ony suld
be offended . . . ?

"Ah, my brethren, let us ask . . . what does His
Presence here, in the lowly form of breid, show mair
than the humility of God. And what is it in the creature
that could revolt against sic humility? Is humility offended
at humility ? Is it humility in the creature that is moved to
anger that He Wha is higher than the highest should for
our sakes mak himsel lower than the lowermaist? Nay, I
trow rather it be that in us that is rebuked by humility.
But it is pride that is rebuked by humility, and it is pride
that therefore hates humility, because it is of the nature of
pride that it will not be rebuked. And therefore because in
the Reality of His Presence in the Consecrated Breid the
humility of God rebukes the pride of man, and that doun
til its first impulse in the secret soul, the pride of man will
deny the doctrine, against reason, aye, against their ain
chiefest professed principles even, rather than abide that
awful, that Infinite rebuke.

"But, mair . . . God, Wha manifests His humility
by his Presence in the lowly form of breid, is also and
nanetheless the Maist High and Holy God. How will
it be with men, sinners, here brocht will-they-nil-they
intil His Presence, compellit to encounter the Divine
Holiness, the Divine Omnipotence – *even to the touch?*
How can they endure it? Awesome even for the soul full
of compunction, contrite, humble, restorit in charity; how
terrible, not to be borne, for the soul full of pride, wanting
in charity, in contrition and the purpose of amendment,
with sins unrepented, unwillant – abune all, unwillant to
bend the knee! What will tak place in the soul of such
an ane brocht here intil the Presence of Holiness, as of
Humility and Omnipotence? He will ken full weil in his
benmaist heart that he suld smite himsel on the breist and

cast himsel doun in abjection of self. But because he will neither abase himsel, nor, not doing it, abide the Presence of Holiness as of Omnipotence, he will *will* Holiness and Omnipotence to be far away from him. There will be a rising up in him of hate – aye, and to violence – against that Presence of Holiness that maks him less than naething, for all his pride. And sae, as he cannot deny the necessity of the celebration of this Mystery, since it is maist straitly enjoined in Scripture, he will devise for himsel – or embrace with joy and a sense of being set free when he finds it professed by others; he will embrace because of its evident 'truth' a doctrine accordant to the whilk it is all but a Figure, and he need have no fear, no sense that he is come to judgment since what he is in presence of, what he partakes of, is but breid. (Wherein indeed they speak truly of their ain sacraments, since they celebrate them unlawfully.)

"And sae the unanimity and violence, nay, the extreme passion, with the whilk all kinds of the heretics assail this doctrine sae plainly taught in their ain Scriptures, point on their very face to pride as their first source, whilk is to say that their rejection of the doctrine is but a *means* whereby their pride and unregenerate will seek to protect themsels against the Divine Holiness, Humility and Omnipotence Whase living touch would shrivel their pride to dust.

"Sae, indeed, it seems . . . Ah, my brethren, this at the least is manifest . . . sae lang as this Presence is in this hoose built by man for God, sae lang will the silence of God be louder here than the voice of man. But if man rid himsel of the silence of this Presence of God, there will be nae voice hereafter louder than his ain . . .

"And now . . . what of Christ's Mother whom also all heretics are agreed in refusing to honour, claiming that they thereby the mair honour her Son – making Him thereby lower than the worst of men, since not even the worst of men will tak pleasure in that their mother is ill spoken of and looked upon . . .What do we read . . .? *'Hail, full of grace, the Lord is with thee; blessed art thou among women!'* Such was the salutation of the Angel sent by God, recorded in the Scriptures. Yet the heretics, although they claim to fulfil all that is enjoinit in the Scriptures, refuse to echo it. Again, in the same Scripture: *'Blessed art thou among women, and blessed is the fruit of thy womb!'* So spake St Elizabeth. But her salutation also the heretics refuse to echo, though it is expressly stated in the Scripture that in speaking thus she was *'filled with the Holy Ghost'*. And Mary hersel – not less, it is very certain, filled with the Holy Ghost – made her reply: *'Behold from henceforth all generations sall call me blessed'*. Here it is maist straitly enjoinit in their ain Scriptures that thenceforward in all times, which includes our ain, she was to be called 'blessed' – and the heretics in naething show mair clearly that they have verily putten themselves outside the company of the true Kirk of God, than in that they refuse to the Mother of Christ our Saviour that title of honour whilk the Scriptures distinctly state was to be given to her by Christians unto 'all generations'. But we ken that already, for they openly mak it their boast. Our question is, *why* do all heretics, in disregard of the practice of the Kirk everywhere in all times and of the prophetic injunctions of the Scriptures – mair, in plain defiance of the thrice-repeated utterance of the Divine Spirit – refuse and also with vehement scorn and anger to honour the Mother of Christ? And what can the answer to this question tell us of the nature of heresy?

"It cannot by ony means be denied that in being chosen by God to be the mother of His Incarnate Son

Mary was exalted in honour above all the children of men; and it would be unreasonable, not to say impious, to suppose that the honour she had on earth has been taen from her in heaven. But the heretics are offended.

"Now what is it in us that is offended at the exaltation of another and moved thereby to anger? Maist certainly it is not humility. Nay, but it is envy, and cannot be aught but envy whilk is angered at the honour gien till another and desires the douncome of all that are exalted ower us. And envy is ane operation of pride.

"But mair . . . Naething defiled can come where God is, and it is certain from her choice and appointment to that dignity that the mother of the Son of God was not less than the maist pure of creatures. Yet we may observe that it is precisely this, her purity, equally with if not mair than the honour gien to her, which moves the heretics to scorn and fury. Now . . . what can it be in us that is offended at purity? I reply that I ken of nocht unless it be *impurity*, for there is nocht else to which purity could be a reproach. If they were not themsels unrepentantly of impure mind they could never be sae offended at the purity of another. And impurity is not itself disjoinit from pride, for it is similarly ane movement of the arrogant natural self disdaining to be restrainit by what would set bounds to its effluence.

"If we have reasoned truly, the unanimity of all heretics in rejecting first the doctrine of the Real Presence of Christ in the Sacrament of the Altar, second, the obligation to honour the Mother of Christ, to call her 'blessed', points to the working of *pride* in them, showing itself in envy, hatred of another's honour or moral excellence, anger in the presence of that to whilk they owe humility, the whilk they are ever unwillant to accord. They do not reject the doctrine and injunction for want of the authority of Scripture, wherein baith are straitly enjoined, but because baith rebuke their pride, their envy and impurity, because of their aversion to repentance in the spirit of true inward worship and abasement. That is to say that heresy, not as regards its multitude of outward forms but *in itsel*, in its innermaist essence, is primarily ane event in the depths of the spirit or will, where it concerns ane operation of pride. If sae, if in its essence it is the will that it concerns, we see how it is bootless to try to understand heresy on its ain terms by the account it gies of itsel, that is, in the mony conflicting doctrines caa'd Protestantism, for these are but systems constructed by the reason, whereas the thing itsel taks place in the spirit and in the will. The true order would therefore be this, that *afore ever the heretics were heretics in their mind through acceptance and professing of their doctrines, they were already Protestants in their heart through pride.*

"Are they such men in their outward bearing as we might look to see them if such be the state of their heart?

"We have all of late days had ower much reason to observe the walk and conversation of them that profess heresy, for they do not hide themsels awa when they may safely appear afore men, and ye will bear me witness that they are all men of a scornful bearing, rapt awa in contemplation of their ain secret greatness, giean respect to nane but themselves, impatient of every other man's opinion, ever exhorting only to destruction of the thing that has been built up, indifferent to every consideration public or private except their ain advancement to dominion. And with their souls filled with impurity, as we may without uncharity conclude since there is little else of whilk they never cease to accuse all that dare to differ from them, and it is out of the fullness of the heart that the mouth speaketh.

"Puir, self-deceivit, self-deceiving men, that understand not nor care to understand what the things truly are that move them in their inmaist souls; and that gang headlong towards destruction, destroying as they gang and dragging others with them! We ought to pray for such, aye, as for the weak and infirm in mind and soul – for truly from this violent, carnal-willed and bloody-minded man wha verily believes himsel a sanct of God 'tis but ane farther step to yonder madman that believes himsel a king . . .!

"Brethren, let us not deal in merely probable opinions . . . The leech cannot cure the disease if he is mistaken as to its nature: nor can we hope to deal with this disease of heresy which in our day ettles to destroy baith Kirk and Nation unless first we truly understand what heresy is, and that in the very principles in the whilk it is constituted as to its inward nature. Our reasoning sae far has brocht us to conclude that heresy arises, in the order of cause and effect, in the first place from pride, that the heretic is suffering from an enlargement of his self, and per consequent of his sense of the limits of his richt and power. If that be sae, if the enlargment of pride in the depths of the soul or spirit is the true beginning, moving the man to acceptance and profession of specific doctrines, *then the doctrines, taken up and professed will be such as will minister to pride.*

"Let us examine the doctrines and see if it be sae . . .

"Tak first this among their chiefest doctrines, that man is althegether reprobate from God as a consequent of the Fall. The doctrine of the Catholic Kirk is that although man is weakened in his will and faculties through the Fall, through Sin, yet his nature remains in its essence guid, as it came from God, and capable of guid, since he can of his

ain will choose to co-operate with God's grace ever offered
to all, whereby indeed he can be truly regenerated. But the
heretics say nay. Accordant to their doctrine the nature of
man under Sin, since the Fall, is evil at its root, althegether
corrupt, utterly incapable of ane guid work.

"Now at the first sight this doctrine does not seem to
minister to pride, since it is unflattering to man. But mark
its effects! We are all of us sairly limited, baith as created
beings and as men in our world, in oursels and as comparit
with others. It is our necessary lot to meet every day mony
that are greater in the land, or holier in their life, or mair
glorious in their gifts than oursels; and we are compassed
about on every side by their works, their memorials and
monuments – as even tak this kirk, whilk stands daily
afore our een a witness that there hae been others here
mair greatly endowed in the faculty of hand and vision
than oursels . . . aye, even of greater piety, for wha can
deny those stanes were shapit with prayer! To them that
accept themsels, the place that has been been gien them
with their limitations, the superiority of others is a cause of
admiration, of thanks to God that He has gien such gifts to
others if not to themsels. But to them that are unwillant to
accept the limits of what has been conferred on them, their
powers and place, what a reproach! – how bitter, what a
cause of burning in their heart, to be reminded on every
hand that sae mony are mair gifted, baith in place and in
person – and hae been mair gifted, for the gifted of the
past have left their evidences around us in the edifice of
their works and of their thoughts into whilk we were born
and are compelled with humility to dwell!

"Now see the effect of the doctrine. At ane stroke
it overthrows the distinction between mair guid and less
guid in man's works and gifts, and evens the second with
the first. For it is very clear that nae guid fruit springs

from an evil root, that out of what is corrupt in its essence naething of merit or virtue can arise, that there can be nae excellence inherent in the works of a totally corrupt and reprobate human nature, or degrees of guidness in works where all works are of necessity evil, and that therefore the giftedness and greatness of some men and of their works are but illusions – not inherent in the men or in their works but only imputed to them by our sinful minds. See what this doctrine does for me, if I am a man that wills not to accept my place – at ane stroke it sets me free from the intolerable burden of the duty of reverence for the gifts and works of others – for the sanctity of the saints, for the loftiness and subtlety of men of thought, for the nobility of great deeds, and for every secular work of man's hand or mind that stands in evidence of the wondrous faculties that appertain to man, albeit they hae been conferred in small measure upon me. For nae langer now are these admirable or to be reverenced, in that they show that man has receivit greatness and has done great things: rather they are to be scorned and derided as the vain works of a radically sinful human nature – to be destroyed even, if I be sae minded, as themselves partaking of sin, as they maun do since whatever is produced of sin maun partake of the nature of sin. Sae it is to pride of self after all that the doctrine of total reprobation ministers, since it dispenses him that haulds it from the necessity of admiration, from the duty of reverence for other men and their works. It is to pride of self that it ministers, for in plain words that he that runs may understand it means but this, that there can be naething and naebody in the world of man greater or mair worthy than mysel, but aa things are reduced to the measure of my ain littleness. *If this particular doctrine does not set me up, it cannot be denied that it at least brings aa thing else doun.*

"Need we look farther for the reason why they ettle to destroy our kirks? A sma mind, full of envy – a soul in the whilk pride of self and the deep-doun knowledge of its littleness are joinit thegether – is bound by its condition to hate the sight of onything mair lofty, mair beautiful, mair noble than it can be or do, will feel it a reproach and a burden not to be borne, and will ettle to ding it doun. They say they destroy the kirks because they are temples of idolatrie . . . They deceive themsels. The true cause is in the springs and deep places of their soul – that they will not endure the scandal of man's nobility. They destroy the kirks, in richt sooth, if they but kent it, out of rage that they could nocht hae biggit them.

"It is even sae with the second chief doctrine of the heretics, that salvation is by faith alane, and not by faith together with love and guid works. What again does this do but bring aathing doun, in the spiritual life, to my ain measure! What does it do but tak away from the saints the merit of their sanctity, and place *me*, here and now, without effort, without onything achieved or even undertaken in the arduous way of salvation, on the same ground and level with them that have wrocht hardest and merited maist! What does it do, that is, but tak awa, aye, from the heroes and giants of the spiritual life, the friends of God that have scaled the heights of sanctity, aa title to ony greater honour than is due to me, though I may be of carnal mind and have striven not at all! Sic maun be the effect of a doctrine that denies all pairt or share in the process of salvation to onything except ane act of confident belief.

"But if these first twa doctrines minister to pride by bringing aathing above me doun to my measure, the third does sae incomparably mair by raising me up abune others. According to the blasphemous doctrine of Predestination,

God ordains some to eternal glory and others to everlasting
punishment, and that not for ony guid or ill they hae dune
or will do, but simply to show His will. It needs no
argument to show how sic a doctrine ministers to the
very heights of pride – for it needs nocht to say, of course,
that they wha profess it aye speak as amang the Chosen
and never as amang the Reprobate. What mair could the
uttermaist of pride conceivably desire for itsel than the
place in this world and the next which these 'Elect' heretics
assert has been appointed unto them by Heaven? (Nor let
us be deceivit by the humility which some among them may
affect. Aa is not humble that casteth doun the ee. And that
humility is nae burden to pride whilk consists in bowing to
a Divine ordinance that has predestinated them to stand
abune their fellows. Nay but – bear me witness here! –
towards you and me their humility consists in saying: Give
place!)

   "They are the chosen people of God, my brethren,
and as such they would fain play the same pairt amang
men in our day as the Jews played amang the ancient
nations. As they are destined to eternal glory as their
irresistible and unmerited destiny, sae equally is it their
lot on earth to wield authority ower aa men whomsoever,
so that there sall be nae government henceforward save
their dominion and all that will not bow doun afore them
nor yet suffer their doctrine sal be putten out of the warld
like sae mony Canaanitish idolators.

   "Pride? Say rather madness! For what is it but madness when baxters and mendicants claim not alane to sit
abune the sancts in heaven but to owercast the temporal
dominion of kings and governments by virtue of ane privy
whisper in their lug informing them they are no clay of
common men but God's Chosen anes afore the making
of the world!

"True, afore men they base not their claim upon that privy whisper. For their authority they hae another doctrine – that the haill revelation of God is in the Scriptures, and only in the Scriptures, and – mark it weil! – that *they* are the oracles of the Scriptures. God, they say, has hidden all Truth in a Buik, and has sealed the Buik – and the keys He has gien to *them*. But again see how it is to pride that this doctrine ministers! Men never claimed sic power as they claim to themselves – naething less than a special revelation, direct from God, to them alane, in a particular spirit or light of interpretation whereby they stand abune all men and alane are able to declare the will of God! Moreover they claim that what truth God has privily gien to them, that is, their private opinion, they hae the right, nay, mair, the duty to compel all other men to receive from them. That maks them – Reformers ever zealous to reform not themselves but others – show as but tyrants in disguise, wishful to play the despot ower men under a cloak of a profession of pure doctrine.

"But let us make yet mair certain . . . If it be pride of self that is served by the gaining of the doctrines, then it will be the satisfactions of pride that would be lost by the losing of the doctrines. Let us therefore ask . . . what would be the state of this heretic, this Elect baker, if he should lose the doctrines of his heresy? It is easy to see that he would suffer on the instant a mortal douncome, to become aince mair precisely what he *is*. Still a baxter – and nane the waur of that! – but nae langer ane Elect baxter with authority from God to knead men and no breid. And sae equally with them all: without their doctrine they could be nocht but simply what they are, as their birth and natural powers hae made them, such men as we ken them . . . among men, compelled to look up to mony of higher place and greater mark; as regards gifts of mind and nature, compassed on every hand by the works of others incomparably better endowed, making them show, as they indeed are, sorry and inferior; as to theology, compelled to remain dumb, as having neither authority nor learning; regarding temporal authority, able only to wield it at hame – if sae be they can rule their ain wives.

"To sic insignificance would they be brocht doun by the loss of their doctrines. Whereas, the doctrine given them, the lowest in the land is instantly lifted up abune the highest, the morally worst is instantly superior to the morally best and with a higher destiny, the dullest of wit is instantly mair glorifeed in his stupidity than the best endowed in his intelligence.

"They may think, puir self-deceivit wretches, that they hae discovered the doctrine hidden from the ages, and that it is the jewel of pure truth that they carry in their heids – but this apple of doctrine grew in Eden, and what they hae perceivit is nae divine light but the gleam of pride, and flicker of concupiscence. It is the effect of the presence of the doctrine in their mind – and I trow we hae neither missed the essence of the matter nor are we uncharitable if we say it is also the *real* even if uncomprehended *cause* of their acceptance of it – that *while without it they are naebody, with it they are gods, having authority ower all men in a world in the whilk there is naething greater – because naething is permitted to be greater – than themselves.*"

THE approaching noise had been growing louder along the street outside and his later words had been more hurried. The great doors of the church stood wide open at the far end, facing him, and some tossing and swirling human mass now swept round into view, and a confused wave of shouting noise rolled into, up, and through the church. Inside, another wave of sound, of scraping and gasping like a beginning of panic, started to rise.

Through the wide doorway a horse's head was seen, mounting the steps, lifting the armoured figure on its back towards the door. Then it was right inside the building, its hoofs clashing on the pavement. It was Pitfourie, his drawn sword in his hand and his narrow eyes under the raised visor darting this way and that.

Now the whole church was filled with frantic noise, a dark noise out of many beards roaring in at Pitfourie's back, the worshippers rushing and scuttling, seeking a way of escape. Shrieks rose to the arches, rebounded along the roof. Pitfourie, now in the middle of the nave, was brandishing his sword and making the trained war-horse throw out its iron-shod hoofs in all directions and give vicious snatchings with bared teeth on this side and that, its eyes rolling and ears laid back. He advanced in this vicious dance, hoofs clashing and scraping, up the church to the sanctuary, and up the steps of the altar, then with the extended point of his sword overset the tabernacle with a loud clatter of hinged metal as it struck the ground. At that the shouting rose in the church like a dark sea, washing to the very tops of the arches and the roof, amplified under the vaulting and reverberating hollowly, shot through with shrieks, and sudden noises of rending and splintering, of windows dashed outwards, images hurled from their pedestals to crack apart and roll upon the pavement. From the ground dust was going up in gouts and spurts, rapidly thickening, a curtain obscuring the melee.

Uisdean MacUalraig in the pulpit was left standing a spectator of all this. One attempt indeed he had made to arrest the cataclysm, crying into the din: "Bethink ye, brethren, bethink ye! Life's but a moment, and judgment is certain! Judgment is certain!"

But it went unheeded. Then he was surprised to see John Tod standing below the pulpit. At once supposing he had come there in the hope to save the church, he made urgent signals to him, to be gone and to escape. But John Tod remained rooted to the spot, below the pulpit, his fists clenched, features upraised, his whole person held rigid in a trembling intensity. Suddenly it smote him that the man's mind was in a different cast and state from what he had expected, from all that was appropriate; and his arm halted in mid-gesture.

"John!" he cried, striving to take in what had already penetrated to the deep region of his mind – though like a lightning-flash that at first confused and blinded him – the paleness of John Tod's face he realised was not from fright but *anger*, and not anger against the mob roaring at its work of desecration, but anger against *him* – "John!" he cried, contorting his brows in his effort to bring the thought forward into the clear light of apprehension, trying in the midst of the now fearful uproar to grasp and cope with it – "John!" – 'something or other like a priest, yet not a priest' leapt from among his old thoughts like a flame illuminating all his mind – he cried, "Tell me soothfastlie! – have you joined yoursel to the heretics?"

For answer John Tod brandished his fist. Then his lips moved, he seemed to shout something, but at the same instant a great window splintered and crashed and there rose an inhuman yell.

At the same instant moreover Uisdean MacUalraig had recollected what was of more importance and dismissing John Tod from his attention turned to descend from the pulpit.

Even as he did so he was conscious of a severe impact, and thereafter of nothing . . .

When he stirred, he groaned. He attempted to raise himself, and at once groaned again. When he overcame the descending vertigo and nausea and opened his eyes it was to stare at first uncomprehendingly at the floor of the pulpit under his spread hands, and the blood splashing on the back of one of them. The effort to recall himself to his circumstances increased unbearably the pain in his head. When it cleared a little he raised himself up.

There was a fateful quiet. The building seemed utterly deserted. A haze of grey dust hung solid in the air. The whole shell had an unfamiliar look: stonework of pillars and arches standing a mouldering, dusty grey. Grey, cold light flowing in unimpeded through the gaping window spaces. The pavement, with scattered, inert mounds of debris, lay under a thick carpet of dust.

Above, through the spaces of the great window, streamers of mist drifted in, billowing forward every now and then in a freshening of the wind outside. When also there came a faint, high whistling dying away on some sharp tooth-point of remaining glass.

Even over the world outside the building, there seemed to hang a strange silence, pregnant with nothingness. Except that now and again, from away over the town, came a faint sound, a faint pagan hooting, hollow and distant, where they must have been blowing into pipes from the demolished organ.

2

UISDEAN MacUalraig roused himself up quickly on his bed. The act of rising to a sitting posture sent an

excruciating flash across his eyes. In this disorder of the
senses he had the impression that the sacristan rushed into
the room with such precipitation that his square dark beard
was tilted sideways.

Then the sacristan had fallen on his knees, and
was bending over as he fumbled at his breast. Uisdean
MacUalraig did not need his agitated whisper to understand the situation and its fearful urgency. Struggling to
his feet he went down beside him on his knees to receive
What was placed within his hands . . .

They had not a moment too many. A sort of disci-
plined tumult sounded below, then many feet mounting
heavily in the house. The manservant broke into the room
with ashen, fear-distorted face, looking over his shoulder.
Already the noise of many persons was in the room
behind. The sacristan took Uisdean MacUalraig under
the armpit to assist him to his feet. Resolutely then,
though still unsteadily, he passed the quaking manservant
and went out into the room beyond.

On his entry a silence fell. He looked first fairly and
squarely at John Tod, who, pale and excited, appeared
somewhat ill at ease, though defiant, then slowly all round
the grim group of which he was the centre, the pairs of
lowering or threatening eyes fixed on him.

At last he said, in a mild voice: "There was no need
for aa this, John."

He put up his hand and gingerly touched with his
fingertips the injured side of his head . . . "I had your
answer already!"

As none moved or spoke he continued in the same
quiet voice, "That's the strongest theological argument
your Protestant Party will ever hae, John" . . . still
touching the swelling of his face . . . "a blow on the
heid!"

Pitfourie, who had been staring at him with nothing more in the expression of his narrow face than a lowering curiosity, jerked his head and burst out with a sniggering laugh.

John Tod, stung, darkened. Casting a blazing glance aside towards Pitfourie, he shouted in his roaring voice at Uisdean MacUalraig confronting him . . . "Get ye gane! Get ye gane! Ye can be schulemaister nae langer!"

Uisdean MacUalraig said reasonably: "I hauld by the provost and the magistrates. Ye have nane authority in my affair!"

At this Pitfourie thrust himself in front of him and announced aggressively . . . "*I* am the p-provost of this t-t-toun! The m-magistrates stand here afore ye! Inglis is the chief b-baillie here" – indicating the merchant whose stout form was planted on John Tod's other side.

Uisdean MacUalraig's expression lighted with understanding. "Ah! siccarly! *That's* what was afore the Council that John bade ring the bells for . . . " He gave the impression of trying to smile. "And *these*" – he indicated the soldiery ranked behind – "will be them that put ye in your office, albeit they are nocht citizens of this burgh."

Pitfourie smiled his amusement. With a movement of his hip he threw forward his sword.

"And *this*," he said, letting his left hand fall gently on the hilt, "was the chief of them."

Between Uisdean MacUalraig's blue eyes and Pitfourie's dark narrow ones was both challenge and amusement.

"If Pitfourie is provost," said Uisdean MacUalraig, "whaur then is the provost?" – looking round the group.

"Priest!" the merchant, Inglis, broke in, standing forward beside Pitfourie, "I rede ye sing doucely!" This man was angry, shaking his head, his face red, at Uisdean

MacUalraig. "The provost, as ye caa him, has the stanes aboot his neb this nicht, and ye will company wi him an ye say ane word mair. The sancts of God hae putten their hand to the plew. Get ye gane! Babylon the great is fallen. Your place is ta'en from ye. Get ye gane . . .! An if ever ye come within this burgh your life is forfeit. For ye will underlie the law against idolatrie as siccarly as God protects the true Evangel. Get ye gane, schir priest – an ye be wysse!"

Uisdean MacUalraig looked at him a little, then slowly round the company again, as if to imprint the picture of them in his memory, still with the suggestion of a smile behind his eyes. Then putting his hand out before him he motioned them aside, and they parted with alacrity to let him pass between, to the door.

As he was moving forward however he felt his elbow tugged and Pitfourie's voice said, low and confidentially at his ear . . . "C-come ower to us, Maister M-MacUalraig . . . Ye can k-keep your p-place syne!"

Uisdean MacUalraig stopped; moved only his eyes round to encounter those close-set ones fixed on his.

"What do ye offer me?" he said, in a conspirator's whisper.

"W-wife!" responded Pitfourie at once, coming closer to his ear, and giving a suggestive twitch to his sleeve . . . "and b-bairns! Ye need nae langer sleep c-cauld! Ye're a wysse-like man," – twitching his sleeve again.

Uisdean MacUalraig had stopped and appeared to be considering. "Man," he whispered, his voice smiling, "ye but offer me trouble baith in this life and the next!"

He made to pass on.

"Think on it yet!" said Pitfourie, still low and confidentially . . . "I hae naething agin ye. I would e'en liefer it were you nor some!"

As the priest moved forward he raised his voice a little
. . . "Think on it yet! It's c- cauld oot-by!"

Uisdean MacUalraig made no response. In any case
all his attention was needed now to command his sensations of weakness, as he walked, somewhat unsteadily,
through the silent men-at-arms.

The manservant had slipped down unobserved, and
awaited him in the shadows behind the outer door, at the
foot of the stairs. When the priest came down he fell on his
knees and seizing his hand began kissing it and weeping.

"Stinking idolatrie!" snarled the stout Inglis behind
him, and with a vicious kick on the shoulder he sent the
manservant sprawling on the stones behind the door.

Uisdean MacUalraig looked round, at the merchant,
then at the soldiery in a crowd behind him on the stairs,
and said quietly . . .

"He was better wi my hand than your foot!"

Pitfourie in the background sniggered again.

AT THE SIGN OF THE CLENCHED FIST

MOVE UP, JOHN

6

PART SIX

H E STRETCHED his legs out in front of him, turning his feet to the blaze. The warmth from the red fire in the midst of the wide fireplace stone-carved all about was less than the warmth within him. This inner warmth, released by that of the glowing fire, bathed him in waves while with arms on the wide arms of the chair he leaned at ease. Turning his head slightly to one side while he pressed it against the high, carved back of the chair, he let his eyes wander up and over the flowered tapestry hanging beside him. The tapestry covered the walls of this snug chamber; scarcely a draught made the figures on it seem to stir in their depicted pastoral. Warmth mounted on the room . . . There could be no doubt about it, all that coldness in the outside-himself, formerly not to be subdued by a fire's heat, had given way, had passed away to warmth that lapped the uttermost of sense, and flowed from verge to verge of consciousness. And that estrangedness that used to be in the 'out-there' had ebbed away and left things solid and familiar all around him: that one-time hardness that, freezing and pressing, smothered the flutter in his breast, had gone, and now – and especially here – he was surrounded by a benevolence in things, turning as it were their mild, accustomed face towards him. He had had to come here – to this room tapestried, all warm from its wide and sculptured hearth, to this wide chair carved like a throne – to encounter and recognise himself, to meet his *real* self, as it were to keep a tryst with his identity. And he felt how *right* he must have been. Howsoever storm-troubled with hesitations those first steps, he now basked in the proof. 'The Truth shall make you free', said the Scripture. And he *was* free, boundlessly free. The Truth had made him free. The Truth had brought him *here*.

True, there was still the hard coldness of a certain steel cap which – it happened now – floated up at times to trouble his beatitude. Pitfourie would look with a long, fixed look of his narrow eyes, at him, then at his daughter, then in a private way, to himself, give his damp snigger; and he would writhe deep-inwardly and for the instant feel as if naked, and know a sense of insecurity – as if he had after all been mistaken about where he stood, and the reality of the situation was in actual fact outwith his grasp. Infuriating above all was the way his wife, his woman, his completing member, looked, fascinated and submissive, at her engenderer then, making *him* – John Tod – feel small, futile and frantic, knowing his husbandly dominance, which should be paramount, insulted by plain sight of a more complete, deeper surrender and submissiveness than he could evoke with all his male evoking. In presence of the radical force of this crude and careless will, steel-encased, the reality of what was between him and the man's daughter fell away, the sanction of their relationship became thin and forceless – they might have been two children, shamefaced, caught in a nasty fault together: he was suddenly made to feel as if he had in fact not been standing on his *right*, but simply on the sardonic tolerance of this 'master.'

But, after all, that masterliness went, for it was not of the household, and masterliness then was his: his with might and force, possessive power – seizing the earliest occasion – to drive out that other masterliness and assert his own, to make himself safe again, indisputably the sole, the sole occupant of his kingdom, in utter and entire possession and free of all domains . . . Ah! after all, *he* knew, he could apply the cure to banish the cloud of that other influence from the sky of his consolation. He was John Tod, and potent; it was thus he had come here . . . And here he was brought back again by such thoughts to the sense of mastery, enthroned in warmth, 'arrived' amidst the solid, un-strange appurtenances soft and beaming all round about him.

But at this point he suddenly stiffened in his chair. From beyond the door facing him, at the further side of the hearth, there had seemed to come a sound . . . as of someone moving. Incredibly, it came again. He sat up, conscious of a stirring over the surface of his head. Slowly, before his eyes, the door opened . . .

At sight of the apparition standing there he started in panic. Then suddenly recognition flashing on him, he leapt to his feet as if pulled up from above.

His exclamation was almost a shriek . . . "*You!*"

For answer the tall, skeletal figure in the doorway, not even looking at him as yet, exploded in a fit of coughing, leaning against the wall, his hand pressed upon his mouth, his shoulders and the upper part of his body heaving. Recovering a little he raised the fingers of his hand languidly in greeting, saying – the old matter-of-fact tone and manner, though the voice was husky and weak – "I come in peace. Have no fear!"

He turned round his eyes, tear-filled with coughing, and seeing a straight, armless chair near him said – with a glance – "By your leave," and sank rather than sat down on it. And at once began coughing again, and went on some little time.

Noticing that John Tod was still standing rigid, looking at him, he said . . . "Sit doun, John," – coughing – "I hae come to speak with you . . . this last once again."

It had been returning upon John Tod, with the dying down of his first panic fear of personal danger, that after all it was he, not this visitant, that moved and stood in security. Nervousness turned to irritation in him . . .

"I thocht ye were gane at last ower the seas!"

Speaking made his irritation rise to anger.

"Ye were *mad* to come in here!" he cried out, flushing up . . . "Ye'll never gang free out!"

The other languidly waved it aside – he was coughing again. "That will be as God wills . . . I hae a monition nanetheless my end is nearhand come . . . But sit doun, John; sit doun!"

Keeping his eye on him John Tod put his hand down on the arm of the chair and lowered himself into it. Sitting, he looked over the extraordinary apparition sitting opposite, with a kind of incredulity, up and down. At the countryman's worn and ill-patched clothes caked with mud here and there as high as the shoulders, at the feet, bluish and wet-looking where they protruded through the burst footgear. Some yellow mud even seemed to be among the fair, dishevelled beard, which scarcely hid the hollowness of the cheeks. A figure altogether disreputable. The eyes – the familiar grey-blue eyes, though sunken and with an inward, fevered or burning look – not resting on him, were passing with a sort of reflective curiosity from object to object about the room. They embarrassed him when they came to rest on his person – with the same

casual impersonality passing over his clothes, even his
broad beard like a flame lying on his chest – even the
hair of his head which he at once became conscious of,
burning in the midst of the room under the edges of
his bonnet, which he became conscious of too, as if it
had suddenly grown smaller and tighter. At last without
halting the movement of that leisurely examining eye,
the apparition that had once been Uisdean MacUalraig
said – he might merely have been unconsciously voicing
a reflection –

"So ye hae hanged the Bishop!"

John Tod started, drawing in his breath: reminded too
unexpectedly of something too recently past . . . Those
voices in the crowd that very day, in the crowd round the
scaffold, railing despitefully on the Saints in the execution
of God's work . . . He experienced again that feeling of
being unsafe . . . threatened. Felt the breath of menace
blow in from outside where there were yet unconsenting
minds all through the land, wills passing to and fro unbent
and unsubdued, eyes that spoke hostility even when the
lips perforce were silent . . . that very day he had seen
them turned on *him*. Why . . . he looked at the figure
with sharp speculation . . . that voice that called out amid
an approving murmur when he would have sought out and
seized the persons of the railers: Let be, Maister Tod! Ye
hae gotten the shepherd! Ye can smite the sheep ane by
ane . . .! Had it been this familiar voice . . .?

He heard himself replying . . . "He was a whure-
monger . . .!" with loudness.

He had the impression he had not been heard.

"And now *ye* sit in his seat!" the apparition com-
mented, with an air of nodding in confirmation of the
thought that was in his mind.

John Tod felt himself ill-at-ease and angry.

"He was ane idolater!" he cried, still more exasperated at detecting a protesting note in his voice and feeling his face flaming . . ."Such should die the death!"

The silence, continuing, still further put him out.

" 'Tis in the Scripture!" he shouted, with a note of roaring.

The figure merely went on looking at him, apparently turning something over in his mind. At last he slightly shook his head as if John Tod's words had reached him and he simply did not consider them worth taking up.

Leaning a little forward and looking at John Tod for the first time, impressively, full in the eyes, he said . . . in a tone whose quietness made John Tod's seem to have been excessively over-pitched and even absurd . . .

"He was an auld man that focht for Scotland!"

John Tod jumped, and could not prevent an exclamation of impatience and contempt escaping him.

The other raised his brows, when suddenly his cough broke forth again. "Ye are honest at least," he said in the midst of coughing . . . "But" – the cough racking him – "your party hae aye been enemies of Scotland."

John Tod felt he had no occasion to engage in the matter: he gave a sort of shrug, and a motion of the head that swept his beard back and forth across his chest.

The figure said, looking at him still, with an eye candid and purged of 'feeling'. . . "It would avail nothing if ye were to deny it, John. It's weil kent to the haill general these mony years gane-by that ilk ane of your chief men and leaders without exception has been in the pay of the English to bring Scotland to their way . . . and to pairt us from our guid freends of France that aye companied thegether with us against the enemy of the freedom of us baith . . . "

He coughed a little in a restrained way, in to himself

. . . "Forbye that, ye were nane guid Scots afore ever the English made work amang you. Come to think upon it, there is scarce ane of your Reforming band that speaks the auld Scottish tongue of the men that made our nation at the first, and that is spoken yet by the maist-pairt amang us in south and north. Except your prophets and preachers that are 'new' men – blawn in from nowhere on the breath of your heresies – ye were aa from the first of the class that were fickle freends to Scotland in the time of our hero Wallace and the first Robert . . . and toun merchants and the like that knap out the English, though it be northern and nocht suddron and spoken by some amang us this mony a year . . . "

"Ye forget, " broke in John Tod, feeling secure again, his beard on his chest, "ye forget the commons. Ye will never deny *they* are with us. They hae gien proof by their works."

The figure had been seized with another paroxysm, his racking cough breaking on the roof. "This hoast . . ." he muttered; and then . . . "Your commons, as ye call them . . . are but that hound-rabble that would bay for onybody that would tak the muzzle aff them – that they truly *hae* proven by their works. They are never the commons of Scotland that aye stood to it against the enemies of Scotland, your paymasters and freends . . . " He coughed a little shortly . . . "I ken ye are aa unwillant to admit onything against yoursels. But there is a buik at your elbock that lies there in contradiction of ye. For your Bible is in the Suddron, the very language of the English. And it is this that ye mak the language of your kirks, and that ye ettle to mak the language of the young in aa the schules of the land . . . Your Kirk is fain, I hear, that the young be weil learit, and it is a point of wisdom in ye, for ye are after all but a few in the land and it is only by the hauld ye can gain ower the minds of the young that ye can mak siccar of your continuing power in generations to come. In guid sooth ye *darena* neglect the learin of the young . . . And the lear that ye will gie them is your doctrines and the language of the English."

A shaft had been loosed, John Tod felt; but so far as he was concerned, at a target that was not there to be hit. Feeling himself comfortable in the situation he said, in a large tone, settling his shoulders against the back of the chair . . . "What matter the speech if the heart be richt!"

The apparition gave him his attention, then continued . . . "It maks a braw sound, John! But what does it mean – in your mouth? Just this, that sae lang as you and your doctrines prevail aathing else is weil lost or cast awa. Ye but confirm my words that ye and your Party care nocht for the nation in comparison with place and position for yoursels and your doctrines. And that will mak ye false and feeble guardians of the nation, for it means that sae lang as your place and the establishment of your doctrines be secured, ye will be ready to cast awa the things of maist virtue and power that mak us a nation." He turned aside and coughed. "But forbye . . . ye ken the auld-word that things are best maintainit by that whilk first brocht them into being . . . and as your Protestant supremacy, whether ye will admit it or no, was set up here by the act and grace of England, sae its nature will ever be to lean to England, as by ane inner ordination for its greater safety. And a Scotland that speaks the Suddron – as the service of your kirks and what ye call your zeal for learin will assure it will – and leans to England, will be, whatever else it be – albeit it may be nocht to you – nae mair the auld Scotland that stood upon freedom and the speech and traditions of our forefathers."

"'Tis but wordly talk, aa that!" John Tod had his own vision of things: the vision was quite clear – and this was outside it. "It's the truth that maks us free. And *we* hae set Scotland free with the truth that is in our doctrine."

He felt immensely free himself saying it. (He was really a pitiful object, this figure so shaken with coughing that one found oneself looking at the floor by his chair almost expecting to see that some dry mud had been shaken out of his rags or from his beard.) Thinking this he only just caught the cough-distorted words . . . ". . . a new kind of truth, a new kind of freedom . . . "

"Aye," exclaimed John Tod, sitting forward, having recalled something to mind, "What is this I heard ye said when ye first began wandering about speaking against Christ's Evangel and us its doctors . . . ? that our doctrines mak a confusion in the soul, and maun be the cause of a correspondent disorder in the world, or some sic thing . . . And look ye weil!" – he sat further forward in his chair – this had become enjoyable; never had he felt so completely *right* and so much at home in a personal encounter, and it struck him that this was the first time of all that he had felt anything of the kind in *this* person's presence – how completely he was liberated! – "Look ye weil! Wha has the best doctrine? *Look* at you, and *look* at me! *Our* doctrine is true, for God has blessed us in the world, and prospered us afore aa men!"

For a moment he continued to see the grey, mud-caked figure – a something of offence, of scandal began to seem to hang about those rags – sitting across from him, quite plain within the room and as it were growing smaller and clearer under his eyes. The next, the room itself seemed to sway unsteadily about him and he found he was holding himself tensed and half-recoiled in his chair. The figure, now again appearing somewhat vague and looming, his hands on his knees in a so-familiar posture that solidly and horribly brought back the closed and finished past, for it was the attitude of a vested priest sitting in the Sanctuary, had leant slightly towards him and at the highest moment of his confident-ness, and in the lowest and quietest tone – as it were very privately – said . . . "Do ye *believe* your doctrines, John?"

"I . . . I . . . maist siccarly . . . I . . ." – in spite of himself, and as it were to his surprise, he found himself stammering into silence at the very moment he meant to be most emphatic. The apparition was looking at him with an attentiveness of waiting, and before he could bring himself up to emphasis again, nodded as if at confirmation of what was in his mind.

"I see ye do not yet *quite* believe them . . . But tak courage, John. Ye *will* believe them. I hae heard that others among you are in like wise afflicted . . .. doubt loupan upon them at times like a robber on the highway. It is because your doctrines are, in richt sooth, the offspring of your ain mind; and the mind, in some fashion, leans to distrust of its ain offspring . . . But tak courage! Doubt will weaken, gien time. Therein lies your hope. Time is passing, we can not halt it, and as day follows after day ye will live yoursel intil your doctrines till they be a part of ye – till your mind and spirit, as it were, be but ane activity of your doctrines. Syne there will be nae mair chance of your being sundered. So hae patience. Doubt will weaken yet. He should gie little trouble in the next generations, wha will be althegether sic men as your doctrines will hae made them, since they will hae breathed in the very spirit of them from their bairn-time, in sic wise that they will be able to see naething whatever, whether of God or man, except accordant til the shape and lineaments of your doctrine – and to ken naething, whether of God or man, except in the measure of the spiritual capacity and apprehensions of them that devised your doctrine."

He broke off. "That is the evil . . . " he said, on the outfall of a sigh, looking away and relaxing his attention to John Tod personally. . . "In the generations to come, insaefar as their souls will hae been formit by your doctrines, everything in the spiritual life maun be holden within the limits of the experience and capacity of Luther and Calvin, the makers of your doctrines, for the manifest reason that naething outside their experience could hae found a place in the systems they devised, since a man cannot put intil his work onything that was not first in himsel. The Catholic Kirk, as ye kent at ae time, never socht to define the manner or the bounds within the whilk man should be perfect, but by the teaching of the highest truth, valid for all, and the dispensing of Divine grace sacramentally to all – Grace, which is simply *power from God* – socht to lift up and sanctifee all men, that is, to perfect them in the spirit, *each after his personal kind as God gave him his gifts*, it being sae that Grace doth not annul Nature but builds upon it, sae that each man is to be lifted up in the power of God to glorifee God by the perfection – and not alane the natural perfection but the supernaturalisation – of his powers and gifts, *whatever they may be*. But ye, because ye deny and forbid everything that cannot find a place in Luther's and Calvin's experience of the spiritual life, henceforth extinguish, suppress and annul, everything beyond *their* capacity for the use of Grace, and limit men in time coming to just sic other spiritual half-grown, turbulent bairns as Luther and Calvin. By sae much, ye lay waste the spiritual future of man . . . Verily, by you the spiritual life is nae mair a gairden filled with various blooms, with odours of divers virtue and perfection, dunged and watered with truth and grace

by its appointed gairdeners, but a desert in the whilk ye
and your brethren walk at large, striking everything that
grows except ae tormented, ill-faured herb whase wersh
fruit comes til its fulness nocht ane handsbreadth abune
the bitter ground . . .

"But I speak overly in the general. . . What was it
ye desired to hear . . . ? What did I mean when I said
that by the confusion they mak in the mind, and the
wrang direction gien to the will, your doctrines maun
as their external effect work for disorder in the life of
men in society . . . ? I mind of saying it . . . " In an
instinctive, unconscious movement he held both hands,
palm outward, towards the fire though it was too far off
for him to feel its direct beam, then clasped the palms
together in his lap. "For example, then . . . man does
not, like the beasts, come into the world provided with
a set of laws written in his members which he needs but
obey in order to live perfectly after his kind. He maun
live humanly, that is, by reason, accordant til a set of
principles or ideals first conceivit in the mind. Now ye,
whether ye fully ken what ye hae dune or no, hae wrocht
a root change in the *meaning* of all the concepts and ideals
by the whilk men, as rational beings preordained to virtue,
maun perforce live. And in sae much as the structure and
condition of society is the outward, social effect of the
dominant concepts and ideals of the men that compose
it, we maun look to see sic changes in the social state as
will correspond to the transpositions ye hae wrocht in the
meaning of the primary concepts and ideals by the whilk
men in societies live."

John Tod only said, somewhat reluctantly – "How
mean ye?"

The other responded, "*Ye* will tell *me* that, John."

He leant his left elbow on his knee and looked at John

Tod along his shoulder . . . "Let me ask ye . . . How do ye conceive Truth?"

John Tod perked up.

"Needs nocht to ask it. *We* hae the Truth. Our Faith is Truth."

The other gave a faint smile, as if hearing what he had expected to hear. He then asked . . . "How then conceive ye Freedom?"

"I hae tauld ye already. It is the Truth that maks us free. *We* are free. Our Faith is Freedom."

"And Justice . . . how do ye conceive Justice?"

"Justice is the establishment of the Truth, which is our Faith" – with condescension – "How else could ye conceive Justice?"

"E'en sae. And Loyalty . . . how conceive ye Loyalty?"

Even more promptly – "He is loyal that holds by the Faith . . . *our* Faith."

"And a right social order, John . . . How conceive ye that?"

John Tod crossed his legs and settled his head against the back of the chair . . . "A right social order is ane in the whilk truth and justice are maintainit. That can only be ane social order under the rule and governance of our Kirk, which is appointed to maintain truth and justice."

"And how conceive ye now Scotland, our nation?"

John Tod, with a snort – "Scotland is but the community of the Saints – it can be nocht mair hereafter."

The other gave a tired smile, and nodded, recognising the answers he had anticipated.

"Now ye maun admit, John, that when ye mak truth, freedom, justice, loyalty, the nation, all the ideals that men live by, equal simply to your religion and its regnancy, ye give to all these concepts a meaning they never had afore."

John Tod shrugged . . . "We give them their true meaning."

"Ye cannot deny, nanetheless, that in your minds all these primary concepts hae been transformed, and hae lost the meaning they had in all time formerly . . . Heretofore men micht dispute about truth, but they aye understood it as something to be established by the mind conforming itself upon its objects; as independent therefore of *my* feeling or *your* opinion – as correcting indeed all judgments that partook of private feeling and preference by submitting them to be judged by the object. The meaning *ye* give is althegether different: simply, *whatever is prescribit by your Kirk*. Likewise with freedom . . . men hae aye kent til now not alane with their minds but in their bodies what it is to live in freedom, and what to be in bonds. Nations also were in bonds when their enemies had dominion ower them, in freedom when they were answerable only to themsels in their ain country and lived freely accordant til their ain traditions as a nation. But *ye* mak freedom equal only to the Protestant religion; *that* is freedom . . . Sae also with justice. Justice was aye supposit to consist in this, that every man – and God first, it needs not to say – should receive his due. *Ye* mak it mean something althegether different, althegether new: simply the regnancy of the Protestant religion. Scotland, too, that was till now a community of men and women of common blood and inheritance working in common under God and by His Will for the informing of life on earth with the especial quality of the 'mind' embodied in their tradition, ye would turn henceforward to mean naething mair than sae mony persons holding the Protestant religion. And upon other sic concepts that men live by and that shape their lives ye work a like transformation.

"Now the effect of those transformations of meaning, though it may be hidden from you, will yet be seen. If your religion be a lie – and I ken it is a lie, if only by the token that I hae seen ye mak it yoursels – then ye mak men to believe a lie thinking it to be the truth, and thereby will cause them to forfeit in their ain life and their societies' the fruits of truth, and to suffer in their stead the disorderly fruits of a lie in the mind; unable to escape the fruits of the lie because believing that their lie is truth. Freedom, for instance . . . our Scottish people will aye cherish freedom mair than life itsel . . . if now they come under your tutelage to indentifee freedom simply with the Protestant religion they will be ready to follow the Protestant religion to the death . . . or waur, to the loss of all true freedom.

"By means of sic a transposition as ye hae made in the meaning of freedom, ye micht gang about to subject our nation entirely to England – as I foresee – while they still supposed they had freedom, and even mair than ever, sae lang as they had – if it was all that they had – your Protestant religion. And for justice . . . under your new transposition of its meaning ye micht work the worst injustice – as your Party hae already done, robbing the poor and giving to the rich – while all rest assured that justice reigns sae lang as your religion bears the rule, and even that there was nae true justice until you came.

"Sae with all the other ideals, personal and social . . . men will nae langer ken under your new dispensation how to realise them, since they will nae langer ken how, richtly, to conceive them. And sae, attempting to realise all ideals in the belief that they are comprisit in your religion, they will reap, it should be manifest, nocht the fruits of these

ideals but in their stead the fruits of your religion. They
will reap nocht but the final effects of your doctrines when
they hae worked out their true nature and displayed it in
the lives of men and societies and nations . . .

"And that these effects of their ain nature and inner
necessity maun be damnable I clearly foresee."

John Tod said, gibingly, "Are ye also amang the
prophets?"

"Nay, John, prophets there be nane amang us, though
amang you I ween there be mony . . . But if things be truly
comprehended according to their nature, sae also will their
effects be foreseen afore ever they be brocht forth."

It all seemed brittle and of no consequence, to John
Tod, and from a man of no account – logic out of a heap
of rags. He had by now quite recaptured the assurance
that of the two it was he that was at home.

Moreover, he knew something, had remembered
something . . . His object now was to keep him there
talking.

"Prophesy til us then!" he said, with taunting assurance, as it were stroking his chest with his broad red beard
. . . "Show us the end of our doctrine!"

"Its end is to be perceived already," said the figure,
sighing, "and maun hae mair and mair enlargement in
time coming . . . For see . . . By your doctrine of faith,
in the whilk ye put doun the intellect and allot its place
to the will, ye hae sown the seeds of division. As indeed
ye do in general and not alane in matters of faith, by the
contempt that ye hae and loudly profess for the intellect
or reason, which ye are wont to call ane whure of the
Devil. Sae lang as the intellect had the primacy, not alane
in matters of faith but in everything that concerned truth,
it was a means of uniting men, of making them *ane*; for
the operations of a faculty common to all, working by

its ain principles which are independent of all, in the apprehension of truth which is abune all and the same for all, could not but work for the uniting of all, and that the mair it was leaned til, the stronger it was in itsel, and the mair it was rectifeed by being lifted abune the passions and all private elements, which by reason that they are private work for division. But ye, heretics and Protestants, when ye mak faith equal to trust and not intellectual assent, and when, owercasting authority, ye choose out to yoursels doctrines accordant with your preference, and when in general ye put doun the intellect from its appointed natural primacy in the apprehension of truth, thereby exalt the personal *will* and enthrone it: and thereby ye commit men to be guided by ane errant private guide which, by the reason that it is private, must needs set men at odds thegether.

"For the will in matters of truth is blind. If it be not guided by reason it maun be guided, or rather led or impelled, by the passions and desires, and as these acknowledge no law save the law of their satisfaction, and that a private and not a common end, the result maun of necessity be the breaking up of the unity of all Christian men, which unity was rooted not alane in a common acceptance of an external authority in faith and morals but in ane universal common assent to the authority of the intellect richtly usit and conformit til its proper ends."

John Tod said: "Aa sic intellectual pish and tush is weil caa'd by Paul in the Scripture 'philosophy and vain jangling'."

"Nay, John, what he that ye with ower-great familiarity call Paul designated as vain jangling was never philosophy pursuing its proper work which is truth, the apprehension of ends, but the sophistical quibbling engaged in for its ain sake, or out of vanity, or for gain, as was much done in these days lang syne. Sic men were condemnit for using philosophy for personal, other-than-philosophical ends – even as ye heretics, as I understand your case, use religion for personal, other-than-religious ends – some of ye, like your freend Pitfourie, in full scornful deliberation; others, the 'sincere' amang you, without kennan clearly what it is that they do."

"Ye may rest easy," broke in John Tod. "We will unite all men with our doctrine and under our governance."

"Will-they-nil-they? Nay, John, even amang the generations to come whom in what ye call your zeal for learin ye will it a chief work to protect from the evidences of the Faith of Christendom to the end that they may grow up to ken nocht but the doctrines of Calvin, even amang them there must ere lang arise those that will turn your principle of the private will against yoursels, that will tak liberty to refuse your authority, til in the end the Christian world be broken intil as mony pairts as there will be individual men able to maintain or impose their private will in the context of things religious amang their fellows."

"We'll tak order with them!" said John Tod threateningly.

"Nay, nay, John, the plain sodjer will ettle to be a captain in spite of ye, and if he cannot be a captain in your army he'll een hae an army of his ain, though it were but smaa. Sic is the human nature ye hae looten lowse, and ye'll nocht govern it for lang. Your persecution will nocht halt it, for naething lifts a man up with less merit or effort of his ain than his public persecution, and such is the force of the passion to be foremaist that mony would be ready to perish by persecution for the sake of that moment of maist exquisite delight when they would be the absolute centre of aa men's een, a moment that naething in them would win for them ony other gait – all the while, it might nanetheless be, in the conviction they were victims on the altar of truth . . .

"And therefore the first and continuing fruit of your religion everywhere it has free course maun of necessity be that whilk the Scriptures plainly say is the fruit of the flesh and nocht the spirit, that is, *sects* . . . sects and the bitterness that is aye joinit to sects. Sects maun multiplee and war thegether even to the death for the power to force acceptance of their private doctrine upon all. Wars I foresee, and the centuries aheid drooned in the blude of the strife of sects; and my heart is wae for those mony and mony thousand innocent yet unborn wha will yet lose life in the bootless fruit of your seed of quarrel. And, the sword apairt, innumerous hearts bruised and broken in their tenderest strings, for the sect sets house against themsels, and there will be father against son, and brother against brother, and dochter against mother from generation to generation . . .

"But there is division far mair radical than opinion that ye work, in the soul . . . In aulden times . . . afore Christ . . . men were aye bound in chains in their minds by the force of ane certain idea, whereby they were able to think of man only as a twa-fauld race. To the Jews all others were but the Gentiles, shut out from Promise; to the Greeks there were but the Greeks – and all the rest shut outside in the wilderness of barbarians. Even the Roman citizenship, though men might pass intil it, was a division across the world of men and a cause of thinking of men as twa – and of treating them as twa. And as ye ken, in all times and generations it was taen as a thing in nature that men suld be of the twa kinds, bond and free. Whatever the principle of division it was the habit of the mind in all auld times to conceive the race of men as, afore everything else, apportioned in twa orders or kinds, ane superior by its nature, ane inferior, ane glorious by its destiny, ane shameful; ane therefore ordered and destined by its nature to bear the rule ower the other, which micht by nae means avoid that governance since it was in its nature for it to be subject.

"That world-auld division of man, with all the oppressions that were bound to be done when there were twa kinds owing naething to ane another save to rule or be ruled the tane by the tother, all that, the pride of the dominators and the groans of the oppressed, and their life without hope because their state was fixed, it was the effect of our holy religion to do awa. In Christ there was nae mair Jew and Gentile, Greek and Barbarian, bond or free: all were made ane Man in the Shedding of His blude for all, ane ae-fauld humankind, of ane equal standing afore God an ane equal hope of heaven.

"Now ye with your doctrine of some that God ordains without merit to eternal life and others ordained without demerit to eternal punishment, hae undone that work of Christ, and by your separating of all men into Elect and Reprobate hae brocht back the aulden idea of man as a twa-fauld race, inheriting a twa-fauld state on earth and a twa-fauld destiny. Man that was made ane by Christ is made twa again by your doctrines. And not only sae, but mair fixedly than ever afore; for the former divisions atween the twa kinds, not even the circumcision itsel, was ever as impassable as the great gulf fixed by God atween the Elect and the Reprobate.

"The necessary effects maun be amang us ere lang. When man became Ane he became subject to the law of luve, without possible exception of ony because all were of ane paternity, all equally redeemed and in hope of heaven: all became answerable under the law of luve for all. But there is no law of luve that can bind twa immutably separated kinds of men, and now again the only justice is that ane should rule and ane be ruled by the other. The Elect, therefore, are by God's ordinance gien the rule at the same moment as they are set free from obligation under the law of luve towards them that will be under them; and it needs nae special knowledge of our human nature to foresee the outcome. The effect of Predestination is to raise up a company filled with the consciousness of God's especial favour, supposing themsels under command from heaven to rule the rest, to whom they owe nothing under the law of luve. But as it happens, the Elect under God's dispensation are maist notably the rich and powerful – or them that ettle to be sae by the exercise of their Election! Moreover they believe another doctrine, that guid works are of nae merit – conversely that evil works are of nae demerit: nane of the Elect can ever be damned for onything he may do upon the Reprobate – that is, in general and in effect, the poor and defenceless – in the exercise of his God-ordained rule ower them, and – I recall to mind – in obedience to the Divine injunction given by the prophet Calvin, wha has commanded ye, I hear, to get rich!

"Mark further that the abandonment of all *inward* restraints on the abuse of inferiors comes in at the same time as the owercasting of the external restraints provided in the Catholic Kirk's ordinances against the oppression of the poor, which it ever enforced against the rich and powerful whenever and wherever it had scope and freedom. Mark all these things and consider the end to which they point. For me, it needs nae garment mair prophetical than these rags to foretell that the effect of this Reformation maun of necessity be sic a setting-up of rich Elect, and sic oppressions of the poor Reprobate, as

have never been since Christ. The voice of the future is
nae cry of joy that rase to heaven when mankind kent itsel
Ane, but the lamenting of a wretched humanity that they
are sundered again intae Twa, and the groans and cries of
generations doomed to toil without hope for the benefit
of God's Elect.

"Nor are oppressions all. For ye cannot set bounds
to the flight of ideas aince ye hae looten them lowse.
They will follow their ain course from mind to mind and
tak up their abode where they will, *alangside what other
ideas they may find there afore them*. Now, the idea and
sentiment of the *tribe* or *nation* is such ane as will be
found in possession when the ideas and sentiments ye hae
looten lowse hae time to gang abroad, and will inevitably
be encountered by them in the minds and spirits they will
inhabit. What will the effect be when they join thegether?
The sentiment of 'the nation' is strong, and it is guid that
it suld be sae, for God did not mak men all of the same
likeness nae mair in their spirits than in their bodies, and
ilka sort He meant to glorifee Him in the perfection of
its nature after special kind. Hitherto all kent they were
members of ane greater unity, Christendom: if there was
strife between nations it was aye strife between brethren,
and in time nae doubt would have had an end when the
Catholic Kirk was mair listened til and charity and justice
had mair honour. Remember that your Reformation has
shattered the bond of Christendom and set the nations
asunder. What will be the outcome, think ye? when your
new-auld idea of the twa-fauldness of man, and the other
idea that ane of the twa divisions is Divinely Chosen to
fulfil a higher destiny and to dominate the other, come
thegether and are joinit til the idea of the tribe or
nation? Do ye not see here the danger fast impending
that whatever remains of what was aince a Christian state

of man, after your Reforming devastations and the wars
of sects, may perish althegether in the resultant wars of
mutual destruction between nations that feel themsels
Elect, 'Chosen' to dominate all others?"

John Tod remained silent. Time passed on, the space
of several instants. The apparition was looking at the
stone-work of the hearth as if appraising the heraldic and
decorative carving . . .

"Ye ken, John, I believe that ye will never root out
from the hearts of men a memory of the distant licht of
freedom aince brocht til the world by the Catholic Kirk,
howsoever dim a recollection of the teaching that in the
eyes of God the slave is equal to the Emperor, that the
poor are even His special care, and that while He will
resist the proud His heart is open to the humble . . . and
therefore in the oppressed a dim consciousness that their
sufferings are unlawful and their oppression contravenes
a higher justice . . . See now that if in consequence moral
indignation of the poor and oppressed should be kindled
at their state it will awake not in a world filled with the
Catholic consciousness, that man is Ane, but in a world
that *your* doctrine and spirit will hae filled with the idea
and the sentiment that man is by state and nature Twa.
(Sic an idea is maist present to the oppressed by reason
baith of the unity of their common suffering making them
feel *ane*, and the univocal witness of the great gulf atween
their state in the world and that of their oppressors, which
are maist evidently of a different 'kind'.) If therefore,
now, the idea of the twa-fauld nature of man – and ane
of the kinds Chosen, the other Reprobate – should be
joinit in the oppressed with their sense that their state
contravenes a justice abune the justice of their society
– should be joinit with their deep-doun recollection of
aince having heard ane authoritative Voice saying the

poor are specially beloved in some Quarter abune the human – an ower-easy transposition would soon mak them the Elect, the specially beloved, destined to rule, and their oppressors, sinning against the higher justice, the Reprobate, wha by appointment should be subject . . . Aince let them become possessed of that idea, and their moral indignation, resentment at lang-endurit wrangs and bitterness of recollected misery – with the inspiring sense that ye hae now of being instruments for the imposition on the world of the order fore-ordained by Destiny – will provide the power on their pairt for a warfare that will be for nae redressing of injustices but the extirpation of their oppressors or the making them the oppressed in turn . . . Suld sic a social war tak place your Elect would perish by a judgment on your ain ideas . . . And wha can say also whether – the wars of Elect nations apairt – the fragments of the Christian and Catholic order that survived your fury and the application of your misconceivit principles, would not be swept awa in that blind avenging flood!"

He paused, and sat looking in front of him. He seemed tired now, and although not coughing any longer appeared to breathe with difficulty. John Tod said nothing. After a little the other went on – more, now, as if reflecting aloud; looking straight ahead, his hands on his knees.

"But all that is in the future . . . There is a seed of mair present ill, forbye strife and blude and oppressions, that ye hae sown with your doctrines . . . and that is the seed of sadness – aye, the seed of despair. And the fauseness of your doctrine is in naething better seen than in this, for the true Evangel was to bring men hope . . . Ye ken that in the ancient days men were sair hauden in their minds under that auld idea that they caa'd *necessity, anangke* as the Greeks had it, and groaned in spirit because they thocht their destiny was written for them in the stars or some sic heathen superstition, and that they strove in vain against a judgment delivered already upon them by their gods . . . And that haill world of auld time burst the bonds of its despair, and casting awa the shackles of 'necessity' rose up rejoicing in the freedom and hope brocht to men by Christ . . ."

He paused a moment; went on even more reflectively . . .

"The sorrow of that bondage to necessity, the sorrowful sense of being bound by ane higher Power to an immutable fate, ye hae brocht back again to be a burden on men's souls. In this also ye hae undone the work of Christ, returning to the auld things that were already done awa, with the doctrine that all men are ordainit to their ain place in the next life afore ever they were born into this, and that nae guid work, nae virtue nor striving can avail to change ocht of our allotted fate, but we are bound utterly and constrainit by a destiny which recks naething of merits as of deserts. How much the mair sorrowful above measure they whase unjust destiny it is to be numbered amang the Reprobate from God, without hope of moving Him nae mair to justice than to mercy . . . But even amang the Elect, if a man had a pairt yet of natural kindness within him he could not but be sorrowful to see sae mony, though better than himsel, ganging their waeful gait to everlasting torments!

"Aye, and your doctrine, not alane that guid works are of none avail for salvation, but that the nature of man is itsel radically corrupt and incapable of ane guid act, and that everything a man does with nae matter how pure intention is utterly vile and stinking . . . what a doctrine to mak a man despair in the midst of his labours in his weary life . . .! Ah, John, this world that we but press under our feet in loupan out of the abyss of non-being

into the abyss of God, but that by the operation of luve
might be turned intil a gairden for the time of our sojourn
here, *ye* hae turned intil a prison, with yoursels as gaolers
ower all men till they be ready to be damned. Fareweil
now to joy! the world is made a weary prison-house . . .!
For myself I declare to ye that even if the faith of Catholics
was ane error, as I weil ken it is not, I would rather dee
now in that merry fault than live my life nae matter how
worldly weil in all the future that may yet be yours!"

He stopped. Nothing was heard in the silence but
the breathing in his lungs. John Tod moved in his chair,
clearing his throat.

Then he got up and stepping obliquely over stood
upon the hearth with his back to his visitant. With his
small foot he pushed over a smouldering coal, causing
a soft crash and as it seemed a faint tinkling. Then he
turned round, and said – his brown eyes snapping about
the room . . .

"Shairly . . . shairly ye hae nocht gotten til the end!
There maun be *other* evil consequents of sic an evil
cause!"

The other raised his eyes to John Tod's face, heavily.
It was seen how the skin burned on his cheek-bones above
the fair, dry beard.

"There *is* another probable end . . . Waur it may be
in certain wise than aa the others" – coughing on the last
word.

John Tod returned to his chair.

"What is that?"

"That men micht tine faith and the inward posture
and formation of religion althegether."

John Tod made a sound indicating incredulity. "That
could never be! To believe is natural . . . and therefore
necessary!"

"Sae it is. Like health to the body. Yet it may be tint even sae. And the lang disedifying of the war of sae mony sects, ilk ane accordant til itsel the sole possessor of the Truth – did it consist of but its prophet and a twa score followers – sae mony ill deeds done in the name of true religion, sae much malice, injustice and absurdity attributed to God by minds of small capacity and little lear making it their ain theology, micht weil at last gie cause to mony to doubt that *nane* hae the truth, that truth in religion may nocht be kent, or even that there is *nae* truth in religion . . . "

He had been looking at John Tod while speaking. Now when John Tod ejaculated, still sceptically – "How would men live their lives syne – without religion?" – he turned away again, and sank into his meditative impersonality as before.

"The necessary effects of the loss of siccar belief are easily foreseen," he said. "They are the loss of all that is founded in belief. That is, firstly, morals. For, religion gane, morals hae nae siccar foundament. With loss of firm faith there maun come the lowsing of ethical as of theological restraints and ane uncertain rule in all that concerns conduct. Men will become their ain judge of what is richt or wrang in their behaviour, if they lose not the sense of richt and wrang in behaviour althegither . . . And – mark this weil! – as the laws and Commandments of God are nocht arbitrarily imposed on man from outside or above, but are *written in his nature* by its structure and constitution, men maun therefore suffer in themsels and their societies the consequents of their actions in breach of the commandments, *whether they only langer richtly ken them to be laws that they break or no*. These consequents are in the discordance and weakness of the faculties of the soul – whase harmony in the strength of correspondence with the commandments of the Creator, which are therefore their ain laws, is the perfection of man. That is, the mind becomes weaker, not alane in its authority but in its operations in everything that concerns judgments, and men will therefore become darkened in their perception of what things are for their guid and the guid of their societies, and judging wrangly will follow harmful courses. That other faculty of the soul, the *Will* likewise, afflicted with weakness, inconstancy and indirection, will hae less power either to avoid evil or to conform itsel to such guid as is still perceived . . .

"I foresee therefore that from loss of belief alane, and the declension of morals consequent thereon – from darkened judgment and the multiplying effect of sae mony acts in breach of the law of God – from this internal cause alane – haill societies micht be made ready to perish . . . Certain they would stand in danger of perdition in that doubt and darkness of the mind, irresolution and enfeeblement of the will, the weariness of life, the hopelessness, aye and despair that afflict societies without faith that hae gane astray in sin, would mak them poorly able to resist a peril from without – as, it micht be, a class or nation that felt themselves 'Chosen' to rule ower all the world."

A little before John Tod had been delighted to think of an argument that should demolish the whole of this. He had merely been waiting till the other paused. Besides, it was necessary to keep him there a little longer. He said, with a tone of triumph, as already seeing himself the victor in the argument – and over such an antagonist . . .!

"In all that ye hae said ye contradict yoursel. If men in the end reject our Kirk and our doctrines, how will sic things arise in later times, being the effect of our Kirk and our doctrines? Answer me that, man of reason as ye be!"

The grey figure did not have the appearance of being greatly overborne by the logical point. He did not even look round at John Tod but went on rubbing the palms of his hands in a gentle, nervous way forward and back over his mud-caked knees. Half-musingly he said, as if disposing of an irrelevance or lesser issue . . . "Tis nocht the doctrines nor your Kirk's governance *in themsels* that will bring these things to be, but the 'mind', the condition of the soul, that engendered them in the first place and that they in turn engender, the formation they gie, to the soul, the whilk they then let loose to work its effects in the world...

"That that 'mind', the same condition of soul that is in you, can be present and active in the world when you and your Kirk and doctrines are not, is evident, since as I hae shown ye the world was full of a consciousness of mankind as twa-fauld, a conviction amang some of being 'Chosen', ower against others that were 'Reprobate', a sense that life itsel was evil and fit to be the ground of nae natural guid, and that the haill of life was ower-shadowed for guid or ill by a destiny that fixed men's ends, and sae forth – everything that marks your ain soul, your ain 'mind' upon life – lang afore ye were ever here, lang even afore the religion of Christians was in the world, or the Christian Scriptures written in the whilk ye claim to hae found all this. And by the same tokens sic a 'mind' and condition of soul could equally weil prevail and remain active in a society that had left your Kirk doctrines by the road or even nae mair professed the Christian name.

"For, ye see, all that – your doctrines and your Scriptures and your Kirk – hae been as it were but a mask putten on by that auld 'mind', that auld formation in the soul, for fear its true, un-Christian face would frichten awa even yoursels in a world that has a lang time been

Christian – just as the same 'mind' wore mony masks of doctrine and mony names in days lang gone by. It is, in fact, this 'mind' that is in you, nae mair auld than of the present time, but a shape and condition of things in the soul, that may form itsel there in ony age, in ony body – but which becomes fixed from ae generation to the next when it shelters under the form and justification of a system of ideas claiming the Sanction of truth, as with your doctrines and theology, and a society or Party to gaird and transmit it, as in your Reforming Kirk. But it is *the shape of things in the soul, the 'mind' upon life*, which is the substance, and therefore fitted to survive the dissolution of such accidentals as forms of doctrines, and kirks and parties. And it is from this surviving shape of things in the soul that the effects are produced that I hae foretauld.

   "For the soul being by its nature active, by its activity limns its ain features upon the outer world of its society, since it can assuredly limn nae others; and sae the character of a human society cannot be other than as the character of the human souls and 'mind' whase activity brocht it into being and made it what it is. Thus, the effect of the activity of men that look on man as twa-fauld – whether they belang to your Kirk or never heard its name – cannot be other than to bring to being in their society a sharp division between twa classes of men; men that act, feeling themsels as 'Chosen', whether they caa themsels Christians or not, will soon in the measure that they have power, bring into being a 'Chosen' class, and another class feeling themselves to be 'Reprobate', for they will be treated as such, and not in charity and justice: men that conceive there is nae merit in guid works will do nane, and will mak for themsels a society free from guid works, that is, full of injustice; a society made up of souls acting in the conviction they are nocht creators of their ain destiny but althegether under compulsion of higher powers, will never be adorned with the marks of freedom, the works of man's free creator spirit, but only by sic works as they conceive they do under the calling of necessity – such as to rule others, or to get rich – or to mak shuin. And sae forth . . .

"That is wherefor it is nocht necessary for men to continue to hold your forms of doctrine or to be ruled by your Kirk, in order to produce the end effects of your doctrines: it is only necessary they be descended by their spirit from men that were aince formit in their souls by your doctrines through being aince subject to your governance. Your Kirk may tine its power ower men to the last iota, your doctrine and theological formulations cease to command their belief and allegiance, or even ony mair to be current among them, yet the formation of their soul remain, the 'mind' upon man, his state and destiny, the way of looking upon life, the lying of their will towards life – and the resultant shape of men's acting in society and towards their fellows – that *ye* will hae brocht back with the establishment of your doctrines."

John Tod exclaimed impatiently – "Ye are beside yoursel! Do ye now confidently assert that aa that ye hae foretauld will surely come to pass . . .? that as ane effect of our doctrine, the reformation we hae wrocht, the poor maun be oppressed, syne at the last rise against their oppressors with violence, that there maun be wars atween all nations thinking themsels to be Elect – as if there were ony Elect save the Sancts! – and that the societies of men, if ony there be left remaining after sic conturbulations, maun dee from within by the weight of their particular and general sins – even though they no longer ken them to be sins – and from despair through the loss of faith and

the sense of truth! Pish, man! do ye now confidently assert
that aa that maun surely come to pass?"

The other turned and looked at him . . . "I am no
foreteller of the future. What will assuredly come to pass
I ken nae mair than you . . . What I do assert is that sic
is the nature of the 'mind', the formation of the soul that
lies behind your doctrines, that engendered them and that
they in turn engender and let lowse, that if and where they
are established and tak free scope sic will be the outcome
. . . maun be, since it follows from their nature as the
stane falls earthwards."

4

John Tod looked his scorn . . . "Sae mankind maun be
brocht in peril of perishing althegether in the end from the
effects and consequents of our Protestant religion . . . or
the formation of the the the 'mind', or what ye caa it . . .!" His
tone pooh-poohed the entire suggestion. He leant an ear
aside, and at once went on . . . "Or is there physic to mend
this sickness?" He had a smallish hand on each arm-end of
the chair and leaning back flicked his eyes under their lids
from the back of one to the back of the other.

The figure was saying . . . "Maist siccarly there is a
cure prescribit that is nocht impotent this side of dissolution."

"Nae doubt your Kirk," said John Tod, without looking up.

"Soothfastly . . . it was for this that our holy religion
was sent into the world, to be the physic for its ills – not
alane to provide the means whereby the souls of individual
men should be sanctifeed and brocht safe hame to their
Eternal Bourne, but also sae that men in the licht of
truth Divinely confided to the Kirk micht live thegether
upon earth in the tranquility of ane order founded upon

charity and justice – and therefore there could never be ane evil state of men out the whilk they could nocht be lifted up again to justice and the hope of heaven by the willant reception of the true teaching and means of Grace which the Catholic Kirk has alane been gien the power and authority to dispense . . ."

"A potent means, i' faith," John Tod gibed, "to cure them in the end of sae vile an evil!"

"But let them *will* their cure," said the figure, "*truly* will it, and not merely wish in their extremity that their state was better than they hae laboured to mak with their uncharity and pride. Syne let them brak their heids on the evidences of the Catholic Kirk's Divine foundation, the authenticity of Her mandate to be the Ane teacher of faith and morals to mankind. They will put themsels syne in the road to be baith enlightened and set free and moreover to receive by the Sacraments the application of the infinite merits of Christ's Sacrifice whereby, if they will, they may be regenerated and the haill race transfigured and brocht back to God."

"Aa in the twinkling of an ee," scoffed John Tod, "by ane miracle of idolatrie!"

"Nay, but accordant to the measure of their guidwill."

"What is the manner of this regeneration?" said John Tod, still with a sneer.

"The manner of it would be by rectification of what ye hae disordered. Consider . . . it was making truth, or Ends, to be be determined by a faculty – the Will – which is by its nature blind, that first set men in violent motion in all directions and in consequent running violently against ane another, like sae mony beasts blinded and driven mad. That faculty, the Will, would be subjected again, as it is proper it should be subjected, first, to the Intellect sae

far as concerns truth or Ends, where ye see the beginning
of the cure of divisions, second, to the rule of luve and
the virtues sae far as concerns conduct, where ye see the
cure of injustice and oppressions. Still mair would divisions
have ane end and sects of necessity wither awa, and the
fruit of sects, the strife and blude, by the recognition of
ane common authority in faith and morals. Again, when
man were aince mair made to conceive of Man as *Ane* by
the Kirk's teaching of the universality of his sonship and
redemption, the aefauldness of the concept of Man in the
active soul would of necessity by its very presence soon
begin to mak him ane and nocht twa in his social world,
dissolving awa the barriers between classes and kinds of
men; laying men again, moreover, under the obligation of
luve and nocht dominance as the universal rule of their
mutual relations. Thus must oppressions cease, and strife
of classes, for there could be nae mair the division of man
into twa kinds. Moreover men would have become subject
aince mair to the ordinances of the Catholic Kirk, which
were ever set against oppression of the poor as a sin sae
grievous that it 'cries to heaven for vengeance'.

   "Nae mair either could there be world-destroying
wars among 'Elect' nations, aince the idea and sentiment of
'the nation' was disjoinit again from the idea and sentiment
of 'Election' – which idea and sentiment indeed in your
prideful sense would be banished from the soul – and men
kent again that they are *Ane*.

   "Dethronit likewise and banished from the mind and
soul in perpetuity would be the conviction of Necessity,
that auld tyrant, and Freedom restorit. For the faith
of Catholics forbids a man ever to believe that he will
certainly be damned, without his will, and teaches with
authority that God is on every man's side and will bring
all to Heaven if they resist not their redemption. See there

the cure of the sickness of despair, mortal to man and as weil his society, by the application of Hope when every man has aince mair in his ain hands the power ower his destiny. And with hope would return joy . . .

"Joy also it is that would be brocht back when men nae langer felt their natural life was evil and man's nature totally reprobate from God, but contrariwise, guid, and though warped with sin capable of being restorit by the Blude of Redemption. With this, the Catholic doctrine of man, he would receive back his mandate to rejoice in the exercise of his natural powers. And sae men would find their road out of your gloomy prison-house intil the sunshine of the natural guidness of things – for things are in fact simple and guid in the world that God has made, and the gloom is in your ain spirit.

"Again, by the restoration of siccar belief – not a pious hope but a certain knowledge, intellectualy certifeed – a world if it were althegither gane astray in doubt would recover the knowledge of its purpose. Further, with the recovery of a sure and certain rule of conduct it would be restorit to the moral life, and begin to lay up again the treasure of virtue, the power in the spirit, the strength of the faculties, and the inward freedom which are the soul's health and the effect of obedience to the moral law, which is the law of its ain being . . .

"That in few words would be the manner of it . . . Just as the disorder that maun come upon a world gien ower to your doctrines will be nae accident of external events, nae fate descended on them from the skies, but ane inner judgment, the reflection in the outer, social world of the disorder that was first in the soul, sae the regeneration of that world will begin by nae application of external salve, but from within. For man, appointed to the Infinite, there can be nae despair, nae mair for his society:

he can only perish by his ain hand, but by his ain Will can
be regenerated. From the instant the soul begins its cure
the external world of society, since it is naething but the
effect of the activity of the soul, maun begin to tak on the
lineaments of that new or restorit inner order . . ."

"I said truly that ye are beside yoursel!" interrupted
John Tod, nettled in spite of himself, having been attending
to the argument in spite of his intention merely to keep him
talking while he on his part kept an ear open elsewhere . . .
"Do ye in sooth believe that a world that has aince receivit
the true Evangel – were it to save itsel from destruction –
would ever turn again to commit whuredom with Popery
and superstition?"

The figure looked musingly straight ahead, moving
his palms slowly with a roundabout motion upon his
knees . . .

"I say only that the physic is provided . . . I cannot say
whether the sick man will apply it to himsel . . . especially
aince ye will hae instructed him weil that it is poison for
him . . ."

He looked at John Tod . . . "I see plainly that the
hatred ye bear to the Catholic Kirk, the common Mother,
sae far passes all bounds that an if it be inherited in like
measure by them that come after, that ye will hae formit,
it micht weil be that in sic last days the sons of your spirit
would reject the ane remedy, and choose rather to perish
than do violence to the bitterness of their aversion, even
for the sake of truth and life."

5

But John Tod thought he heard at last what he had been
listening for, and abruptly withdrew his attention. Behind
the door on the opposite side of the hearth from that by
which the visitant had entered, there had been a sound.

Now a sound of movement came again, with a dry clatter. He leapt out of his chair and rushed to the door, throwing it wide.

"*In here!*" he roared, and was all at once shaken with a rage he had not at all felt while sitting listening.

There was a sound of someone approaching. John Tod, suddenly red to the eyes, pointed a violent finger, shaking in emphasis, at the figure sitting in the room . . . "Gaird him with your life!"

With an unmistakably casual, strolling air a stocky man-at-arms came through the doorway. He looked not round the room at all but at John Tod in a cool, detached way, resisting his excitement, examining him with his eye.

"Till I be back . . .!" boomed John Tod, "Your life, mind!" – and was gone.

The stocky man-at-arms turned his head over his shoulder and looked after him: then – when there had come from below a muffled, slamming sound – hooked his heel round the edge of the door and closed it behind him with a vigorous movement of a casual leg and stood himself somewhat astraddle in front of it, barring egress. Sticking his thumb down inside his belt he raised himself slightly on his toes, and letting himself down again on his heels turned up his eyes under the snout of his steel cap, and began to make them – his lips forming a pushed-out 'o' in his dark-brown moustache and beard – travel all about the room . . . the tapestried walls, the chairs and tables, the carved fireplace with the Bishop's coat-of-arms – turning himself slightly to look at it round his left shoulder. Then back again to looking all about, with widened eyes under his elevated eyebrows, rocking himself gently backwards and forwards and appearing to whistle silently through his pushed-out lips.

Gradually the rocking motion ceased: he came to rest, heavily. His sturdy limbs seemed to settle into the floor. Only then, attracted by a paroxysm of coughing, did his eye cross over and rest on the man he was supposed to guard, sitting on the chair well into the room at the farther side of the hearth. He was only a grey heap on the chair. As soon as John Tod got up he had leant forward with his chest resting on his forearms crossed above his knees, and now was shaken with continuous spasms, his face turned downwards. The man-at-arms could see the hollow at the back of his neck deep-sunken between the two sharply upthrust shoulders. He half-shrugged and changed his position, shifting his weight.

Once or twice after that as he stood idly there his eyes in passing rested impersonally on the grey figure. On one occasion the face was visible: the coughing having subsided, he had pushed himself up to a sitting position, his hands pressed on his knees. Twice the soldier's eyes rested indifferently on the face, and passed on. But suddenly their wandering was arrested. A slight shock seemed to pass through him. His eyes narrowed in an intense inward speculation, then slowly, with a sort of wariness or suspicion, moved back along their course. A moment they rested on those unconscious features with a sideways watchfulness, then clung to them in incredulous recognition.

"*Dhia nan Gràs*, God of Grace!" broke from him in an intense whisper . . . "Is it you?"

The figure realised he had been addressed and looked up, and seeing the man-at-arms bending towards him, with mouth agape and wide eyes in his weather-beaten face, got up and came a few paces forward, looking closely.

"Oh.. . . ." he said . . ."You, Crucisanct!"

The man-at-arms regarded with a sort of fascination the features that now seemed to be floating near him.

"King of the World!" he whispered. "Is *this* what they have done to you!"

He was about to say more, but appeared suddenly to come to himself, drew himself together with an energetic look. "Now . . . take heed . . ." he called out warningly in a resonant voice. "I cannot let you go . . . Take care!" The sound was dry as he pulled the sword in its scabbard forward – towards the grey figure as it were – taking at the same time a half pace backwards. "I . . . I . . ." Resolution went out of him again . . . "Why ever did you come here?" he burst out, red with embarrassment.

"Have no fear," the other reassured him. "Indeed it matters little now. My end is not far off . . . I feel that . . . if it be not my sickness that is disordering my head."

"Think not little of me . . .!" – the soldier's tone was protesting now, his air apologetic – "Think not little of me, I pray you!" He was both exasperated and uncomfortable, his eyes seeking escape this way and that. "What can I do? I no longer hold from the Abbey, you must understand that. I am Pitfourie's man now . . . our new Abbot!" – with an audible sneer.

"I altogether understand, Crucisanct . . . And there are the wife and the little ones." The grey figure spoke quietly, looking down at a portion of a foot protruding from his shoe, his voice very hoarse.

"Yes, yes," agreed the other, "the wife and the little ones . . . A man has to think about that. But don't think . . ." – he was all protesting eagerness now: the sword was pushed back – "don't think I am with *them*! God, who is with *them*? Even in the town here the craftsmen are all against them, though the merchants, damn their stinking pride, are for them . . . But what are the common men

to do? It's for Huntly to move, or Angus, or . . . the men
among the hills. Let them move to take order with the
traitors and these . . . bellowing mouths, and . . . you'd
see. But . . . without leaders we'd be like sheep. And,
as you say yourself, there are the wives and the little
ones . . . For the present, a man can only do what he
can . . .

   "But, *hist*!!"

   The sound of a sudden entry came from somewhere in
the house. The man-at-arms stepped aside from the door
and assumed a wooden expression and posture, looking
straight in front of him. The grey figure stepped back
and took up his position quietly near the chair he had
been sitting on. Some persons entered the room behind.
There was a gruff order, a clatter of arms. The door flew
open and Pitfourie strode – the air plainly written on him
of impatience to be done with something he was in against
his inclinations – right into the room, not in armour, a
light sword flying out at his hip. John Tod, at his heels,
between his black gown and cap was as red as the slashes
of Pitfourie's velvet. One would have said that words had
passed.

   Pitfourie took his stand in the middle of the room,
glanced with casualness at the grey figure of a ragged
countryman standing there and then turned his narrow
face all about as if looking for someone he expected to see.
And not seeing him he wheeled and gave John Tod, who
was still speechless, a flat, inquiring stare from impatient,
narrow eyes.

   At the same moment the attention of the grey figure
was attracted to the man-at-arms. Something violent was
happening to his face. With his right knuckle he was
rubbing his right eyebrow hard, while at the same time
his left eye was giving a series of prodigious winks, after

each of which both his eyes seemed to flick rapidly in the direction of the door by which the apparition had first appeared. The latter gave a quick look of understanding and with a leap went from sight. The man-at-arms raised a loud warning shout and leaping across the hearth dashed through the door in hot pursuit. Immediately there was a shout inside the room, an armed clatter, a tremendous crash.

At the very instant of the man-at-arms' disappearance through the door Pitfourie, enlightened apparently by his warning shout, had leapt long-legged after him. And immediately there was another shout, a reverberating though softer thud.

After a second's silence came a stream of screaming curses. John Tod was left standing all alone in the room, his resentful anger contending in his face with a new uncertainty and even moments of alarm.

A sound of slow movements started in the silence in the room beyond and continued for a time. Pitfourie came slowly through the door. He was holding the flat of his hand across the middle of his face, and John Tod started back. His clothes looked dusty too. Right up to John Tod he stalked and over the top of his hand again gave him that long, flat stare. A trickle of blood from his nose was running out between his fingers.

Shortly after, the man-at-arms emerged with a wooden expression from the other room, and with an air as unconscious as his newly acquired limp was emphatic, passed across the hearth and went slowly, painfully, out through the other door.

His jerkin might well have started to smoke between his shoulder-blades by the look of John Tod's that followed him . . .

5

"Oh, John! you nearhand tint your dearie!"

He replied with but a grunt. The security of a bed
shut-in, warmth of bed-clothes, comfort of a woman's
body, had not this once achieved their solacing effect. That
encounter had unsettled him . . . brought back the past too
much, to press upon his spirit. He had that sense of *looming* again, of being tied, almost of suffocation. He moved
his head back and forth on the pillow, freeing his throat
... Those ponderous tomes were opening again, over his
head, more and more of them, opening forever: there
was no end of them. And words were passing over him,
more and more words streaming forever backwards and
forth, too high, although he strained after their meaning.
And voices . . . those gravely intoning, subtle, disputing
voices . . . how he had *tried* to understand what they were
talking about! It was their subtle modulations that made a
wall to make him feel shut out! Worst of all . . . worst of
all the encounter had brought back upon him once again
that intolerable Weight that had formerly crushed him to
annihilation . . . Oh, that filthy, idolatrous Act! The Mass!
Why was It still in the world? . . . Stifled and burdened
where he lay, he tossed restlessly, unable to be calm . . .

Yes, and even the oppressive sense of the militariness
of fighting men was returned upon his spirit. By way of
Pitfourie's sensed unresponse to his own fervour in the
matter of securing that opposed figure fluttered in from
the past, and whose disposal would have settled so much
that was still menacing and a threat – the unmelting iron
of Pitfourie which simply turned his unction back upon
him become thin and silly, made the flow outward of his
will check and waver and break against his. Pitfourie was
immovable, had nothing in him of turning towards John
Tod – no matter how frantically and with what continuous

force he flowed out towards him, at or against him. He always had – had very much at this moment – the chilly feeling that Pitfourie was far away from him, in a different country, not with him in zeal, at bottom without interest in the great affair – or even in *him*. Very chilly at the moment was the (not unfamiliar) impression which came over him, that Pitfourie was more turned towards that other one, that now disreputable and outcast figure, so far as their respective *weight* with him was concerned. He was in a mood to believe, now, that Pitfourie must have known that ragged figure was he whom all had been seeking everywhere – a ragged countryman standing in the middle of the Bishop's chamber! It was a trick between them! That hard-as-iron man-at-arms fell inside the outer room, and caused Pitfourie to fall over him, by arrangement to let the other one escape! That inscrutable look of Pitfourie's over the top of his hand . . . He felt sure now he had been laughing at him. *A-aach*! sometimes he *still* felt it: they were all against him – just as they had always been!

He had, however, one comfort and defence against all that, here, under his hand. He turned towards her – he was beginning to get comfortable now in any case – with a note of interrogation in his next grunt, taking notice of her.

"Near lost ye . . . ? how was that?"

But while she was relating how the bull, got loose from Sanderson's croft, had pursued her and the maid as they were returning along the road . . . they had run screaming through the bushes . . . he caught little of the excitement of the breathless tale. He had passed on again . . . This was Pitfourie's daughter, horse-faced though she be, and blemished, nor young . . . *his*, who had never in his life been troubled or assailed by the seductiveness of seductive women, but could never so much as hear the name of a woman of gentle birth, irrespective of her age or person,

without a prompt stirring of his senses. Her arms were on
his neck . . . Pitfourie's daughter, one of the gentry, those
'others' – and *his*; appointed by God Himself to him, by
God's ordinance, which cannot be gainsaid, appointed to
submission, and to him alone!

The tale came to an end amid smothered exclamations.

Ah, there was nothing . . . nothing in life . . . like
his pulpit self, he glorious in power and freedom, raised
on a point of eminence which no one else could share
with him, from which he thundered on those below with
complete abandon, utter unrestraint, without stint or pity,
till he felt all, even the high-born, the spawn of truculent
soldiery, shudder under him.

It was a deep sleep, penetrating with re-creative warmth
and restfulness to his very marrow, from which he felt
himself dragged up to consciousness. From the reluctance
of his coming to himself he knew that something very
definite must have woken him, and he lay, unconscious
of his limbs as yet, listening in the dark.

Down below there broke out again a knocking, muffled but imperative . . .

He was just putting down his candle in the room
with the tapestry when the yawning, half-clothed servant
ushered him in . . . the same stocky man-at-arms that had
been there the day before: and there was so much of
seeming menace in his form as he came through the door
that for a moment John Tod felt apprehensive, standing in
his bare feet, and had to tell himself that the situation was
such-and-such. No doubt it was simply the man's trade.
In any case he was standing now practically on the same
spot he was occupying yesterday – though not particularly

respectfully, his thumb hooked into his belt, looking as ever, solid and iron-hard.

"What brings ye at this hour of the day?" asked John Tod. The room was in fact filled with a very thin, cold light of dawn, enough to be gradually quenching the beam of the candle. The man-at-arms stood gleaming dully – a shadowless, solid greyness. No doubt it was this thin, morning light, and perhaps some reflection of it under his helmet, that was causing the eyes to seem to hold a weird gleam, in the face which looked ashen and slightly vague in outline above the darkness of the beard.

"I thocht ye would be blithe to hear . . ." he said, that weird gleam stirring in his eyes, his resonant voice sounding metallic in the grey of morning . . . "He's awa."

"Awa?" echoed John Tod.

"He's by wi it," repeated the man-at-arms, and as the other still gave no sign of understanding, slightly turned his head and gave a sharp, sideways, indicatory nod in the direction of the chair whose straight shape was still standing in the same place, beyond the hearth, well into the room.

"Nay!!" shouted John Tod, between affirmation and incredulity. As the truth gripped him he trembled: then shouted in ecstasy.

"And I misdoubted ye yestreen! I misdoubted ye!" He lifted up his hand . . . "Oh come and see a true sodjer of the Lord! Come and see ane weil-affected to the Cause of our salvation!" – driving his fist into the air above him, roaring – "Yea, verily, wheresoever is preached the true Evangel, there likewise will be tauld this that ye hae dune, for the comfort of the Godly and a terror to idolaters! Weil dune, guid and faithful servant! Enter thou . . . but . . . but . . ." – his face changed; the fervour went from him – "Nay," he said in a moment in a changed voice, "it should nocht hae been sae! Ye were to tak him, nocht to slay him . . . An this be bruited . . ." – he was nervous, apprehensive – "I blame ye not, I blame ye not!" – deprecation fluttering in his hand – "'Twill be accounted unto ye for righteousness. But . . . gie nane occasion til the heathen to rage. Mony there be yet that lust after the auld idolatrie, and lookit on him as a bricht brand of hope. We maun gie nane occasion till we hae time to tak order with them . . ." He pondered a moment . . . "Quick!" he said . . . "Bury him afore the bruit gangs forth! An it be kent he was slain by our hand . . .! Though 'twas a godly deed . . . But, quick . . . bury him . . ." – with urgent gestures.

The stocky man-at-arms, growing up into clearness and solidness under his eyes in the mounting light, remained unmoving and an unmoved spectator of all this excitement. He said stolidly, very matter-of-factly, "Ye miss the mark with baith your praise and asweil your fears, Maister Tod. I never slew him. God kens I could never hae slain him."

"Wha did, then? Wha did slay him?"

"Naebody."

"But . . . but . . ." – he looked his disbelief – "He was no that far through yestreen. If he be in sooth deid I ween he has been slain!"

"I said not he was not slain."

"What mean ye? A slain man means a slayer." He started forward . . . "Or do ye tell me fire cam doun from heaven?"

"Nor yet fire from heaven, Maister Tod," said the man-at-arms with a kind of laugh. He seemed to hesitate as to what he was to say. "He maun hae taen the road by Sanderson' s croft . . . and that bull . . . that bull . . ." – his hand moved as if he were scattering something about – "He was weak, ye maun understand . . ."

Now, faltering into silence, he was completely clear and solid-human in the light. If John Tod had been looking he would have seen him shake his helmeted head, and the motion of his solid arm, and this time he could scarcely have misinterpreted the gleam that passed behind his eyes.

But he was not looking. He was gazing straight before him in a vision.

"The finger of the Lord!" he whispered . . . "I thank Thee, O Lord! I thank Thee! Now naebody can blame us! Oh how wondrous are Thy works! That hast putten it intil the heart of the brute beasts to work the establishment of Thy Kingdom!"

Suddenly he wheeled about and strode to the wall, and stood with his face to it. The man-at-arms looked in amazement at the shaking of his shoulders, as he waved him to go out with a hand gesturing behind his back. Looking back as he went out he saw him still standing there against the wall, and the candle pale and useless in the midst of the flooding grey light of the new day. John Tod had turned to the wall to hide the violence of his emotion. Never till that instant had he suspected how that personality, now gone out of the world, had all his life confined his own. That big man had been intimately bound by association to all that had stifled him within, forbidding him to soar. (As if he had not always known – he thought, with bitterness yet – at how little they estimated him, though nothing was said, only they withered him with the condescension of their civility – and that undisguisable tone of their speech that instantly denoted that they were speaking to him across the boundary of a vasty realm he remained without.) No single subtle voice that he knew disputed any longer over his head . . . Such vain jangling it had all been! All gone, and forever! No disputation could there be henceforward but that he could lead in, no argument but on ground that was his own. He was gone, and had taken with him – this above all . . . above all! the last weight of personal recollection and association binding him to the influence of that hateful Act, that annihilating, unhuman Mass, whose lourd effect would ever make but a peripheral antic of the greatest prophet's Word.

Henceforth no act of worship but that he would stand above and conduct in person. Never again to shiver shrunken at that Stone, little before the people. No longer to feel overshadowed. Now for all time coming to assume his pulpit self. And resound, gigantic!

Heaven was unoccupied above him, clear to the uppermost.

He was free—FREE!

FINIS